THE CRADLE OF STONE

By Jeff Pratt

Can't Put It Down Books

The Cradle of Stone

ISBN: 978-0-9994623-0-0

Printed in the United States of America

Published by
Can't Put It Down Books
www.cantputitdownbooks.com
An imprint of
Open Door Publications
www.opendoorpublications.com
Yardley, PA 19067

Cover Design by Eric Labacz
www.labaczdesign.com

This book is dedicated to my mother
for her sweet spirit and her love of animals—
To my father for his courage to do and say
what is true and right—no matter the cost—
To the "Lenape Way" for the understanding
that upon this earth and in the heavens all is alive,
connected, and sacred within the heart of the Great Mystery.

TABLE OF CONTENTS

PROLOGUE

Some stories end. Many are lost. Some just fade—and die.

Other stories, a few, go on and on. Just when such a story is about to die it lives again, like the flame released from a fading ember placed upon a bed of dry bark. Both story and ember require a human heart to tend and nurture them—and the deep need to honor and preserve what is true and right for those who follow.

Both story and ember provide warmth, without which one might perish in the cold.

This is one such story, a story of long ago, of this present moment, and of times still to come. Three boys in the dawn of their manhood, live the story. They do not know each other, are born and live in different times, different worlds. Yet, though each travels his part of the story alone, all three love the same Earth, honor what is sacred, and join hearts to carry the sacred ember to a place of rest, and relight the fire.

~~~

This story begins not with a boy, nor a fire, but with a stone, a Great Stone as tall as two men. The broad surface is dark gray under a clouded sky, but when seen beneath the sun or moon it takes on a silver sheen. This stone is like no other in the valley, though other massive stones rest near the river. Those stones are soft, born of the crumbling ridgetops high above. This stone is as hard as seared bone and smooth as skin. The People speak of it as a stone warrior from a lost tribe, one who has journeyed far. This stone is sacred to the People. They call him *Ahsen*.
~~~

Sacred, too, is the thin trail of water which falls upon *Ahsen.* The water spills from a crack in a rock face which juts out over the Great Stone. Like the stone, the water has journeyed far, from the sky to the Earth, through soil and stone, then released once more to join the air and play in the sun. The People speak of the waterfall as *Ahsen's* ancient bride, long separated, now ever-returning to the arms of her husband. She is called *Sukpehelak.*

A shallow pool of crystal water swirls and shimmers at the place where *Ahsen* receives *Sukpehelak.* And yet as he receives her, he releases, again and again, as her waters pass through a notch in the stone and fall away. The People believe the soft voice of the waterfall sings the words of Old Spirits. The People call this place *Sansun Mimens*, the Cradle of Stone.

Here, if the heart is open, one hears in the whisper of the water that which is true and right will never die, and true actions, like waves on the water, move ever onward till they reach the shore.

Just now a boy and his canoe journey through the night. The stars and moon are hidden, and a cold spring rain falls across the land. Nestled on his lap the twin halves of a freshwater clam shell enclose a fire seed, a single ember sheltered in ash.

And so the new story, born of the old, begins.

Part One

CHAPTER 1
NIGHT JOURNEY

He knew the way even in the darkness. The rain was cold, and it had been falling steadily for a long time. Dipping his paddle softly into the black water he made his silent way, like some forgotten spirit of the night.

The rain hissed as it touched the river. He looked for landmarks to judge distance traveled, but the darkness revealed none of her secrets. Twice the canoe raked the bank as strong currents twisted and doubled back. And once a tree, undercut by early spring floods, moved with him in the darkness, brushing his arm with its outer branches. The boy slid his finger along one thin branch and touched each swelling bud. He whispered a prayer for the fallen tree and paddled on.

At last he reached a sharp bend in the river, a place he knew well, and he drew close against the bank. Pulling the paddle from the water, the boy placed it at his side, then set a warm shell alongside a rawhide packet. He covered both with his deerskin cloak and reached out to the roots and branches to pull himself along. As he reached for his next handhold he found the opening. Here the current flowed against him, pushing him back out into the river. He took hold of the paddle, plunged it deep, and entered the narrow channel.

The darkness deepened. The current quickened, pushing hard against him. Snags, twists in the channel, conspired with the flow, but he fought his way until the push of water slowed and he could catch his breath. He pulled hard on the paddle one last time, and placed it across his lap. The darkness, like the current, was softening. First the tip of the canoe, then the water just ahead rose from the darkness. The rain was now but a whisper on the water. The canoe drifted on until it came to rest near a raft of cut willow saplings. For the first time on his night journey, the boy smiled.

"*Temakwe*! You are here, just as I hoped you would be...*Wanishi*, my friend."

And, though he spoke his thanks softly, the distant slap of a broad tail on water spoke to him in greeting. All through the journey no life had shown itself. Now here, at the entrance of the Great Marsh, the beaver were out, working in the darkness.

The boy looked up to a sea of thinning clouds. The rain had passed and the darkness unraveled enough to reveal a dim island only a few boat-lengths ahead, a little island made of wood. The boy guided his canoe alongside, lay down his paddle, and reached for the shell. Placing the seed of warmth gently in a niche between sticks, he pulled himself from the boat and onto the lodge of *Temakwe*. He climbed to the top, looked out over the marsh and up to the lightening sky. He spread his arms wide to the Four Directions, and his words flowed into the spring night, to the Sky…the Water…the Earth.

"*Gitchi Manito*, I thank you for holding fast to me on this dark journey."

"*Temakwe*, my gratitude to you for granting me this place of rest. I feel the presence of the little ones beneath me. They hear me, and they stir from their sleep. Mother, tell them not to fear, that I mean no harm and will soon be gone."

He turned to face his village, now so far away.

"My old friend. My guide. My true father—I thank you for your kindness, your wisdom, your love. I thank you for your spirit, now too strong to be held by a body so old, so tired. Though I would wish to be at your side through your last journey, in the arms of my first journey, I know you travel at my side. Your words have brought me here; your spirit urges me on. I will be faithful to my promise."

His hand moved in the direction of his eyes, as if to touch, and then hold, the hand of another.

His body slumped and his arms dropped to his side. The boy was very tired, and to gather strength, he knelt and closed his eyes. He breathed in the moist air, invited its life into him. All around him were the beaver, the spring-wakened fish, the turtles rising from the mud, and the faint twitter of night-flying birds moving North.

"It is all here," he whispered to the night, "and now it begins again."

When he opened his eyes he looked upon a far different night. Through a veil of cloud the moon, a tipped cradle of light, shone upon the Great Marsh. Before his eyes lay a sea of silver-gray broken here and there with islands of flattened winter reeds and shoals of floating mist.

"*Kitakima Telemaskek*," he breathed. "I have returned. And with the help of *Piskeweni Kishux,* sun of the night, I will find the path through your heart to the place I seek."

The Great Marsh lay silent. The moonlight brightened, dimmed, then brightened again as narrow bands of clouds, like the ribs of a deer, moved across the sky. The night was warming, and swiftly, the little islands of mist grew, and between them rose more. Once he had retrieved the shell, boarded the canoe and pushed away with his paddle, his path was gone, lost in the rising mist. After just a few strokes he could see the bow of the canoe and no further.

"So this is how you greet me, *Telemaskek.* I would hope at least you would not oppose me. Now I find you have swallowed me. I could rest here and await the dawn. But my friend spoke the words—'this night, under the moon, at the sacred place—' I cannot rest until I set my feet upon the stone. I cannot rest even then—I must..."

A rush of wings, the brush of a feather across his cheek, then the cry, "Killdee! Killdee! Killdee!" first at his ear, and on into the gray wall of mist. He touched his face, then peered into the shrouded night.

"*Kwuskwuti!*" he called. "Have you returned alone? Where is your wife?"

Again the call, shrill and urgent, "Killdee! Killdee!" just above the boy, and then again just ahead. He reached for the paddle. Again on his bare arm he felt the touch of wings. With the third call pointing the way he thrust the paddle deep into the still water, then again, then once more.

He set the paddle across the canoe and held his breath.

Again the call, still ahead but a little to one side. He took hold of the paddle and turned the canoe, brushing the twigs of a button-bush, and then the call once more, now closer and to his other side. In the heart of the Great Marsh, enmeshed in a sea of mist, the boy's ears were his eyes, and the killdeer was his guiding star.

The canoe moved on toward the lonely cry that drew the boy through meandering channels between islands of button-bush and fallen reeds. The silence between the calls slowed his pace, but he never stopped, and, again, then again, the call from the unseen flier pierced the fog and pointed the way.

"Killdee! Killdee-e-e-e"

He turned his head to the ghostly call and his words held wonder.

"Are you my helping spirit?"

His paddle made no sound as it touched the water.

"Or are you just a little bird, tired and alone—lost—like me?"

A quick flurry of cries, "Killdee-e-e-e! Killdee! Killdee! Killdee-e-e-e-e!"

Then silence. Then the faint, deep beating of a distant drum.

"There is no village near," he whispered. "The Old Ones. They are here. They know I am coming, my friend, just as you said they would."

Another sound, like rain upon a faraway forest. The sound was a distant sigh, the breath of the Earth.

"Sukpehelak!"

Once again, the boy smiled. The bird was gone somewhere in the mist. No more cries, for now there was no need. Looking to the sky, he spoke to *Kwuskwutis*.

"We are alone. We are weary. But, my friend, I was wrong.

We are not lost. May you find your mate. May you both find your home. *Wanishi*!"

He paddled slowly. The slow beat of the drum, like that of an ancient heart, faded, as the voice of the falling water rose. The rich marsh smell gave way to that of wet stone as out of the mist loomed *Ahsen*. The boy bowed his head in gratitude. Having directed the canoe to a secure cove near the stone, his hands reached down to hold the shell, still warm and dry.

He lifted his cape and wrapped it around the shell and rawhide packet. The food pouch he slung over his shoulder. His hand touched the knife and tinder-horn at his side, then quickly up to the medicine pouch beneath his buckskin top, close to his heart. To the side of the great stone lay the remains of a tree top blown down by a summer storm. The twigs snapped sharply in the moist air. Opening the cape the boy placed these alongside the shell, and enclosed them deep in the folds.

The boy had been here only once before and had found there was no easy path to the crown of the stone. The one that he knew he took now, along the rear of the stone where it met the steep upslope. The climb had been hard on a day when the ground was dry, but now, on slippery ground in the darkness of the moon-shadow, he twice lost his foothold and fell back. This time he tore off his moccasins and threw them up to the top of the stone. Digging his toes and fingers deep in the soft earth the boy crawled his way to the place where earth and stone parted. He reached to place the cape and food pouch on the stone shelf above him, found a handhold and pulled himself to the top.

Here the mist was thinner, the moonlight stronger. His breath slowed as he gathered himself. He opened his ears to *Sukpehelak*, knelt and touched the face of *Ahsen*, and turned his eyes to *Sansum Mimens*. The trembling pool at his side caught and broke the moon into shards of soft silver. The waterfall whispered secrets of The Old Ones. *Ahsen* grew warm beneath his hand.

He reached down to the tinder horn, opened it and withdrew a small handful of shredded elm bark; the inner bark was dry and soft as skin. Of this he formed a cup. The stone beneath his other hand was now warm and dry, and here he placed the little nest.

Above the nest, twig by twig, the boy fashioned a tepee in which he left an opening. Reaching for the warm shell, he lifted it from the deerskin and placed it at his side. A cool breeze flowed down the ridge and he pulled the empty cape over his shoulders and drew it tightly around him.

"My friend, I am here. I have prepared the fire-house. For the rest, I will await a sign from you that it is time."

The boy drew up his legs and wrapped his arms around his knees. The moon had passed its highest point, and its bright crescent joined the river of stars flowing across the Western sky. The Great Marsh below him, still cloaked in mist, spoke to him with many voices. The distant call of the killdeer, now paired with another, told the boy the little bird had found his mate. The splashes from the spawning fish, the child-like voices of otter pups as they followed their mother, the chuckle of the wood frogs as they awaited their brides—he heard them all.

He looked in the direction of the distant village, and his eyes filled with tears. An old man's heart, on this vibrant spring night, was fading.

"Why must you go? I have no wish to be alone again."

His eyes searched the sky until they rested on a little point of light just above the moon, and his heart found a home among the stars. And, just as he had done on so many nights, alone and troubled, he whispered to the distant light.

"I am called *Alonqua*—Star—just as you are. Stay with me a little while. The night is old, so I won't be long."

Alonqua lifted the shell and placed it under his cape, close to his heart.

"I will tell you the story of my name."

CHAPTER 2
CHILD OF THE SKY

Perhaps it was only a cloud passing across the moon, but the star brightened a little, and Alonqua smiled.

"*Wanishi*, I am grateful you know me, and that you bend your light to me. My friend said many times that we are part of the stars, and the stars are part of us. He told me each of you is an ancestor. I believe this."

Alonqua held his cupped hands out to the little star as if to hold the light and bring it to his heart.

"Do you know my friend? He is a good man—and he is old—and he will die this night. I speak to him, but his spirit prepares for a journey, and I do not think he hears me. My father, my mother—are in the spirit world. My father gave me my name, and my mother blessed his choice. I will tell you the story of my name. Though the story is known to my people, I have never shared it. Now, here, I need to tell it myself.

"I will begin as my friend would begin, each time he told a learning story."

Alonqua cleared his throat, straightened his back, squared his shoulders, and spoke to the little star nestled in the heart of the Western sky.

"Hear me, my brother! May my words be the bridge that connects our hearts!"

"I had lived seven winters when my mother told me the story of my name. On a late autumn night, the night of the first snow, she took me in her arms and said word had come that my father was dead, killed in battle. He died with his leader, Tecumseh, the Shooting Star, the Panther of the Sky. But that is another story—it may be you know it.

"She had planned to share the story of my name in the spring upon the return of my father. To comfort me, to console herself on that cold night, she decided it was time I knew the story of my birth and my spirit home.

"She told me I was a summer child, and that my birth was hard, as if I wanted no part of this world."

The star called out to Alonqua, as he sometimes did when he was lonely. And he heard his words in the voice of water touching stone. *Stars are born, too, Alonqua, and before you go on, I wish you to know we, too, struggle to be born, and as we live, we burn. We feel pain. And we die just as you.*

Alonqua watched the star as it faded slightly and brightened once more, and again he smiled as he would to a friend with a shared secret.

"I cannot doubt that, my friend. And I understand there is much we share. Even so, it is hard to think of you crying out on that summer night. It is hard to see you comforted by a mother's arms."

The star was silent, and Alonqua continued.

"The helpers had just left the *wikewam* to tell the village of my birth. My mother, weak as she was, sang to me. I cried. My father reached to me and carried me into the night, saying it was time to receive my name. I cried louder. As he later told my mother, he spoke to me sternly that such wailing was not fitting for the strong son of a warrior. That did not impress me. I had good lungs, and I was unhappy—and my cries split the night.

"As my father recalled, we had reached the river path when we came upon a wide clearing in the forest. At that instant I was silent. My father stopped and looked at me, terrified I was no longer breathing. He recalled my eyes were wide open to the clear summer sky. His eyes followed mine, and there, like a river of silver dust, flowed *Opitemaken*, the White Road. His eyes returned to my face; my tears were little stars.

"When my father returned and placed me in the arms of my mother he said I was to be called Alonqua Sippu Kikku Aschowen, He Who Swims in the River of Stars. My mother agreed. She held me close and prayed to *Manito*, just as she would come to pray every night, that I, Alonqua, would always be one to shine in the darkness."

That is a good story, whispered the star.

A deep splash below *Ahsen* drew Alonqua's eyes from the star. His hand moved to his heart, then to the medicine pouch.

"*Wanishi*, my friend. But I find now I must share something more. This will be much harder, but is a part of the story—my story—and it will be good to share it on this long night."

He unwound the red cord that bound his hair and held it out to the star.

"This is all I have from the man who gave me my name—a Shawnee warrior who knew him retrieved the cord from my fallen father and brought it to my mother, who passed it on to me. I last saw my father the morning he left the village to go to war. His face was painted red and black, and his eyes burned cold. No one in the village joined him, and his words of farewell were hard like stone striking stone. He touched my hand and my heart before he melted into the forest. He was a hard man, but he was a protector made bitter by the loss of our land. I would have wished to know him better. I know the love in his last touch, and in his choice of my name."

Alonqua placed the gift around his neck, then opened his medicine pouch. From deep within its folds he found the cocoon of the dream-flier, the ghostly green moth of the summer night. Within the silken pouch rested a tiny feather the color of a cloudless morning sky. He held the feather out to the star.

"Do you know *Chihokepelis*, the bluebird? This feather was his gift to my mother to soften her grief."

Alonqua gathered himself. His next breath came hard.

"This feather was her gift to me the day she died. Please linger just a little while with me, while I tell you of that day."

The star did not speak; neither did she turn away.

"Autumn passed and Winter bit deep and held on. The other

women in the village advised my mother to take another man, that she was still young, and that there were men who had interest. But she wished for no other man. My mother loved my father; he was the one, and the wound of his death would never heal. Though the village shared the little food it had with us, she worked hard to earn each morsel, grinding corn and acorns, mending shelters, gathering wood. But always she found time for me.

"Spring brought warmth and food. But it also brought fever. Seven children died of it. Three men, all young. Three women, one of them my mother. She fought hard; five days, five nights she burned. She fought to stay with me—tired and hurt. But on the last night I saw the light leave her eyes, and I knew the fight was over, and that I was alone.

"I had lived only eight summers, autumns, winters, springs—but my only thought was that I wanted no more of this life. I released my mother's cold hand and ran out into the night. It was a night like this, misty and cool, the clouds thinning. I reached the edge of the village and entered the path that led to the river. I wanted to cry, but there were no tears. My heart was a block of ice.

"I tripped in the darkness and landed hard on a log along the trail. The pain was a relief. I just sat there, watching my breath turn to mist. I wanted the night to take me."

Reaching his hand across to his shoulder, he continued.

"Then from behind a firm hand gripped me here, not harshly—firmly. And I heard a voice, a kind voice I knew well.

"The voice said to me that the world is hard, and that for one so young I had been called to carry more than my heart could bear. He came around to face me and asked me to stand. He searched my eyes, touched my dry cheek and revealed to me the sorrow in his own eyes that cradled the sorrow in mine. He held me close to him, and for the first time in days I released my tears.

"No one needs to tell me what happened next. I was no newborn. I opened my eyes to look up at the man. All around his shadowed face flowed the silver river of stars. The pain was not gone, but I knew then I wished to live. Again the old man placed his hand on my shoulder and guided me home.

"His name is Mawenteh. He is the heart-gatherer. On this very night he said to me that I must not grieve, that his body is only a husk and must be cast away, and that his spirit will live on. But before I left his side and entered the night I took an ember from his fire. I placed it in a shell and brought it here. Also here is the packet, a gift from Mawenteh's wife, River-bird Woman. I am here as he asked, and I have what I need to help his spirit find its way in the darkness."

Alonqua turned his eyes to the little rock shelf which held the nest, twigs, packet, and shell. Reassured, he spoke once more to the little star, now low in the west.

"My story is done. And you will soon be gone. Before we part I need to tell you that Mawenteh has been my father, my guide and my friend. That cannot change. Still, it is very hard."

The star once more called to him through the voice of the falling water.

Alonqua, as you know, I was born, feel pain. I know what it is to be lonely in a way you cannot understand. You see, I have never had a father to protect me, a mother to hold me, no friend to teach me.

Alonqua reached out his hand as if to touch his distant friend.

"Little Star, that is true—but neither did you have to see them go."

Both are hard paths, said the star.

"Yes," replied Alonqua, "they are."

CHAPTER 3

FIRE IN THE NIGHT

Alonqua watched as his night companion touched the ridgetop across the river. The star flickered there—twice—three times, as if she did not wish to leave; then she was gone.

The night was old. Only a little time remained before the dawn. Alonqua leaned toward *Sukpehelak*, listening, waiting. The call of *Ghokos,* the owl, drifted from a wooded island across the marsh, a wavering call, haunting and lonely. Alonqua reached for the shell, placed it on his lap. He felt a tickle on his bare forearm. A spider had found his warmth and was feeling her way toward his open hand.

"*Xaluputis!* No sooner do I say goodbye to my Sky Friend, than I bid welcome to another. You are brave to rise so soon after this hard winter. I fear your food still sleeps."

Xalaputis found the hollow in the palm of the boy's hand, and there she rested in the warm harbor.

Alonqua looked from his hand to the sky. A breath of wind touched his face—that strange wind that sometimes rises just before dawn. All around, above and below him, powers moved and gathered for the coming day. *Temakwe's* work was done. The family, both young and old, were in their lodge, eating heartily the gathered food, tasting the sweet, spring willow sap. Birds in the low bushes along the marsh awoke and shook the dew from their wings. He heard them twitter softly to the fading night and then fall silent, waiting for the dawn.

A shadow moved across the stone. Looking to the west, across the marsh, Alonqua watched the stray cloud crossing the crescent moon. The wind rose and blew his hair across his eyes.

"Mawenteh's heart no longer beats," Alonqua whispered to the little spider nestled in his hand. "Can you feel his breath? Can you hear it? Can you see it in the mist of the waterfall? It is the breath of my friend as he releases his life, and his last breath now joins mine—and yours—and all that live."

Alonqua stood and raised his hand to an overhanging branch.

"*Xalaputis,* I would linger with you, and I know that a warm hand softens the chill of night. But now this hand is pledged to what I came here to do. Stay close, my friend."

The spider crept across his palm, up his thumb, and onto a thin branch where she came to rest.

"*Wanishi*, *Xalaputis*, I will not be long."

Alonqua reached down for the shell, lifted it from the stone and held it to his heart. The shell was warm; the ember lived. He turned and spoke the words as he had learned them from Mawenteh whenever an old fire is reborn and becomes new.

"I offer this seed of fire to the East, the place of new life, new beginnings, the place from which flows the breath of the Creator."

Alonqua once more touched the warm shell to his heart and turned, this time to the Southern Sky.

"I offer the new fire to the South, from which rise the winds of summer which embrace us with the warmth of a mother's arms."

Turning to the moon, now low in the sky, he spoke once more.

"I offer this gift to the West, to the land of our ancestors and of the old ways which live still in the glow of the setting sun."

He turned then toward what Mawenteh had said to be the true home of the Great Stone, *Ahsen*.

"I offer this warmth to the North, to the power of the storm, to the peace which rests under winter snow, to the cold spirits that guard what is sacred."

Alonqua turned again and looked toward the distant village

where there lay an empty shell upon a bed of furs next to a cold fire.

"It is time, my friend," he whispered. "It is time to plant the seed."

With his knife, Alonqua cut the binding which held together the two halves. He lifted away the upper shell. He gently blew on the ashes within the lower shell until all that remained was an ember, corn-kernel in size—still glowing, still hot—resting on a bed of pearl.

His hand trembled. Alonqua breathed deeply once again, and the hand steadied and reached toward the opening of the tepee of sticks and the soft dry nest within. A tilt of the shell and the red seed lay on the bark. Alonqua blew softly on the ember, and a curl of smoke rose. Another breath, and a flame licked the air, like the tongue of a little snake. He placed more bark upon the new fire and the flames rose to meet the wood. The seed from Mawenteh's fire had burst open, and this new fire, born of the old, blossomed upon the stone.

He lifted the packet from the stone and opened it. One by one he removed the four little bundles and placed each alongside the fire. Then he knelt, reached out and held one of them, and spoke.

"May the voice of the cedar awaken the guiding spirits and guide them here to this sacred place. May the smoke ward off those spirits that dwell in darkness."

Alonqua opened the bundle of cedar shavings. One by one they entered the flames and sprang to life, crackling, sending bright sparks high above the fire. The smoke rose, clean and pure, and was carried away by the rising wind. Reaching for the next gift, he bowed his head and closed his eyes.

"Sweet grass, the flowing hair of our Mother Earth, bless the fire and this place with Her love for all Her children, and those children to come."

Alonqua placed the short braids of grass upon the fire and breathed in the sweet smoke which billowed from the flames. He placed his hand upon his heart.

"Mother, I feel your presence, and I am thankful you are

here."

As the sweet grass melted into the little fire, he reached for the slender bundle of sage. Alonqua held the tip in the heart of the fire until his fingers burned and the smoke appeared. He stood and placed the smoldering leaves just above his heart, and with his other hand guided the smoke down, up, and along his body.

"Spirit of sage, cleanse my spirit and prepare my heart. Heal the wound of loss, and give me strength to do what is true and right."

Placing the remaining sage on the fire, Alonqua reached for the final bundle, dividing it into short moist strands. Once again he knelt before the fire, now ebbing away into a gathering of embers.

"Sacred tobacco, grant me worthiness to do what I must do; with your spirit comes the dawn of all true actions. With your spirit I invite the spirit of my friend."

The breath of the tobacco rose and the wind shifted and carried the smoke to the East, then to the South, to the West, then the North.

Night held on. The moon-cradle rested upon the Western ridge as the fire burned down to a single ember. Alonqua lifted the empty shell from the stone and scooped the new fire seed from the bed of ash.

"Mawenteh, I have done all you asked of me. I have used the words you taught me, and my heart feels their power. This last request I will do, and though I do not understand it, I will trust it, as I trust you with all my heart."

Holding the shell with the ember, he approached the pool, knelt, and tipped the shell toward *Sansun Mimens*.

There was no hiss as the ember touched the water. Instead the pool embraced it, held it, as a mother would a child. Alonqua leaned out over the pool and watched in wonder as the orange star spun in the heart of the swirling water. Then his eye released a tear, only one. The teardrop joined the pool; the star brightened, then rose, still spinning, slower now, skirting the edge. And then, passing through the notch, the star fell — and was gone.

Breathless, Alonqua knelt at *Ahsen's* edge and scanned the

dark water for the lost star — for the ember that would not die.

"Can I have seen what I have seen?" whispered Alonqua. "Fire—and water? But I saw this glowing coal grow brighter in the heart of *Sansum Mimens*!—Mawenteh! What have I seen? Fire and water are foes! An ember from your fire—the sacred water—can it be?"

Alonqua closed his eyes and cried out "Mawenteh! Mawenteh! Where are you?! Speak! Speak to me of this wonder!"

His words split the night. Across the marsh, *Temakwe's* family paused in their work and looked to the east. Wakening turtles stirred and opened their eyes. A raccoon prowling the bank, froze, then backed away.

"One word! I ask one word! Mawenteh!! Ma-wen-teh! Where is my friend?"

Silence was his answer.

Alonqua trembled as a reed in the winter wind. He lowered his head, his voice again but a whisper.

"*Shielintam*—I am sorry, Mawenteh. It is wrong of me to call you from your journey to the River of Stars. I saw something I did not understand. And you are not here to help me—and I miss your voice. And I am sorry, *Kitakima Telemaskek*, and all who live here. I did not mean to alarm you with my selfish cries."

Lifting his head, Alonqua opened his eyes to see a gathering of moonlight far out upon the water.

Alonqua looked up to the source, up to *Piskeweni Kishux*.

And then he remembered, there was no moon. The moon had set when he started the fire. What remained of her was an afterglow, no more.

If Alonqua wished once more to cry out for Mawenteh, the wonder of the glowing water silenced him. Heartbeat by heartbeat, he watched the glow spread out from the center in golden rings, as if a moonstone fell in a pool of light. But like ripples of water, these, too, began to weaken and fade beyond the power to see.

Alonqua rose—very slowly—as if to test his legs and the Earth they stood upon.

And when he found the words he did not whisper—nor did he cry out. He spoke as one who has seen a wonder—been touched by the Great Mystery. He spoke as one who does not know an answer, but trusts there is one.

"Mawenteh, I asked where you are. I now know. You are here. Your spirit—your light—is here! The ember from your fire! Words you taught me—the sage, the cedar, the sweet-grass and tobacco! *Ahsen! Sukpehelak! Sansun Mimens!* And I am thankful you are close…and yet, so far away."

In the pre-dawn darkness one would have to be close to see the darker shadow cross his face, or to hear his voice tighten with doubt.

"But, Mawenteh, if you are here, I have a question. Why choose to light your spirit fire here? Why do you not join your mother and father, place your fire alongside theirs in the River of Stars? That is what I would want—to see my mother—to see her eyes—to touch her hand—to hear her sing! That is what we all want! If your spirit lingers here, I fear you do this for me. I do not want that! Better to be on your star journey! Better for me! I am alone, Mawenteh! Again! You are free! Go! Tell my mother I am well—I will find my own way—I do not need you here!"

Shocked by his own words, Alonqua fell back from the stone edge, and into the waiting pool. Scowling and sputtering beneath the drenching flow, arms and legs flailing like a turtle on its back, he scrabbled his way out, first falling back twice more.

Alonqua, still frowning, stood up slowly, a trickle of blood from his shin, and a bruise on his backside. He watched the growing puddle of water at his feet, shook his head twice, and laughed. He laughed a long time, long enough to warm himself and ease his shivering, long enough to feel the shadow pass.

"Mawenteh! If I wondered if your spirit is here, there is no doubt! Your spirit is here, and I think your old body, too. I think you pushed me!"

"Alonqua smiled, a wistful smile.

"Yes, Mawenteh, I remember what you told me—many times. Angry heart, foolish mind, blundering body. But I have one more question for you. Why do I never remember this before

I fall on my *wasiti*?"

Kneeling before Sansun Mimens, he reached down, cupped his hands, and drank. His pounding heart eased and his breath came to him slow and deep. Behind Alonqua, high above the ridge, darkness was softening. The night had flown to the West, and from the East flowed the light of a new day.

Alonqua stood and held his hand in the falling water, then touched his hand to his face.

"*Sukpehelak*, I feel your pure spirit once more flow through me. *Wanishi*! Your tears cooled my anger. And *Sansun Mimens*! Haha! What were Mawenteh's words? Yes! He said, 'of all the gifts of The Great Spirit laughter is most sacred.' I did not understand—I feel my bruises. Shiver in my wet clothes. My heart is clear. Now I understand."

He lifted his eyes to the stars—then down to the stone—then out to the four directions.

"*Gitchi Manito*—I am alone. And there are times I am far away from you. It is when I am afraid—and then my fear becomes anger. *Manito*, I ask your patience. I am a slow learner. Anger will find me again. I will fall again. And again. I ask you not lose trust in me when I stumble. You cannot stop my fall. I ask only you watch me rise."

The Eastern sky was filling with light. The songs of the birds greeted the dawn. Alonqua approached the brow of *Ahsen* and sat down as one would with an old friend.

"Mawenteh, I am thankful you know my heart so well. I ask forgiveness when you would tell me I have no need to ask. This night is no dream. I will not awaken and find you at my side. You are gone. And you are here—I cannot hear you. But I know you speak—I must walk this path alone. But I long for your guiding hand—I wish you a star journey. But I am thankful your spirit is near. Mawenteh, my heart is pulled this way and that way! Will I find the place between?"

Alonqua's voice trailed off. Lowering his head between his knees, he shook it back and forth while taking in a long breath. Turning his eyes to the glow of the rising sun, he gathered his words, and released them, one by one, to the new day.

"Mawenteh, this circle—our circle—is done. Another begins. I have done what you asked. Your fire—your spirit—lives. Here. I do not know why. If it is to watch over me, I ask you to look away sometimes. If it is to guide me, I ask you guide as you have before—without my knowing. I ask you—I ask—nothing. You know. This is my path."

Alonqua was very tired, but he rose from the stone with arms wide and he breathed deeply the promise of the dawn. His canoe was just below, awaiting him at the edge of the Great Marsh. Above him was *Xalaputis,* the hopeful spider, already hard at work, spinning her web in the early morning light.

"My path—mine alone—begins—now."

CHAPTER 4

HEALING TREE

In the dim light of a new day Alonqua swept the ashes from the stone and gathered up his few belongings. The sun still lingered well below the ridgetop, and as he looked out upon the marsh, tall plumes of pearly mist rose and spun slowly in the dawn breeze. He wrapped his deerskin cape around his shoulders and found his way down the side path to the canoe. He turned and rested his hand upon the base of the cold stone.

"I will return to you, *Ahsen.*"

He looked up to where the crystal water tumbled from the spring high above the Stone.

"And to you, *Sukpehelak*, now I must go to a place far different from your gentle ways. And if I do not go there, I can go nowhere else. I will earn no spirit name. *Aptachuteh*, I come to you with fear. I will leave you with courage."

Alonqua turned to the canoe, eased himself in and pushed off to the North, to a region of the swamp few knew well. Paddling slowly, his eyes fixed straight ahead, he came to a place where the reeds disappeared and the gentle current of the spring-fed marsh died away. No spring arrowroot nor marsh lilies were twisting their way to the light. No early midges were breaking the water surface and joining the air. Ahead, the marsh was clogged with a scattering of broken trees, old, rotting, abandoned there by floodwater long ago. Near the heart of *Kitakima Telamaskek,* a short paddle from *Ahsen* and *Sukpehelak*, on a warming spring dawn, lay an island of winter, of death and decay.

Alonqua paused and looked across the dark water until he saw it.

"There you are. It seems nothing changes here. Mawenteh named you well, *Aptachuteh,* the Place of the Frozen Heart. And you are still here, waiting for me."

In the near distance, no more than a long stone's throw away, rose the twisted branch, writhing up from the lifeless water like a dark and painful thought.

"The feathers once scattered here are gone. But still I see them. It is time they leave my heart."

He closed his eyes and waited, his mouth set in a grim, hard line.

"Do you remember, *Aptachute*h, when I was last here? Yes, I know you remember. There is nothing dark that escapes your memory. You recall that my mother had died, and I fought the pain of her death for many days. Mawenteh helped me through much of this fight, but there was a spring morning, much like this one, when the hurt overcame me."

Opening his eyes, Alonqua pulled the paddle from the black water and laid it across the canoe.

"That morning dawned with only one thought—*Kitakima Telemaskek*. I wished to hide, to be far from any human face. *Aptachuteh*, I now know I was drawn to you as a moth is drawn to a dark flame. And here, at the edge of your darkness, I watched the duckling, perhaps a moon old, too curious to stay with the other little ones still close to their mother. I saw the swirl in the water just before the little one was pulled under and devoured."

Alonqua's tone turned bitter, as if each word had the taste of that dark memory.

"It was *Pamputis*, the old turtle with stone jaws, who tore that duck to pieces, leaving only the few scattered feathers which I see even now. I wished at that moment only to kill *Pamputis*, to strike him hard with my paddle, to summon the killer to choose one more worthy of a fight. But even then I knew the truth my friend spoke to me. *Pamputis* kills to live, and that no blame should come to him. He said I would do well to remember that bold ducklings have short lives."

The boy looked toward the West where the village lay.

"Mawenteh knew my anger was not for *Pamputis*. And soon I knew it as well. My anger was for the Whites, the eaters of salt whose bullets pierced my father, whose sickness took my mother. He taught me anger can hurt no one I hate—only myself. A good lesson; but now he is dead, gone, like my mother and father. But *Aptachuteh*, it is anger that I want. Anger has heat. My heart *is* empty and tired, frozen like yours. I match your heart with my own."

With the growl of a wolf he thrust the paddle deep, pulled back with all his strength, and thrust again. But his hard stroke slowed as he entered the heart of this empty realm. Whatever fragments remaining of the living marsh had given way to *Aptachuteh*. The murky water and gray mist sucked the light from the sky and dragged it under. Alonqua struggled to keep moving. But there was nothing ahead nor behind, no vision, no sound, no scent that held life. All around lay the rotting remains of what was. He once more looked back to the sacred place, now lost in the dark morning mist.

"Little Star!" he cried. "*Kwuswukis! Xalaputis!* My friends of the night, where have you gone?

"Father! My mother! Speak words to me! Tell me your spirits live! Reach to me! Touch me!"

Warm tears turned cold as they fell upon his hand.

"And Mawenteh, my friend who spoke always of trust. I do not know this word. There is nothing left to trust. *Aptachuteh!* Speak to me of death, of loss! These I know!"

A drowned branch caught the canoe and held it fast. Alonqua jerked the paddle from the water and struck the darkness hard, again, and again, then again. Fountain after fountain of foul water fell back upon his head, shoulders, and arms. He struck and stabbed until the water seethed and foamed. The branch at last released its grip and his canoe broke free. Alonqua slumped over, gasping, breathing like one newly born.

For a time he listened to his heart, pounding like the drums of the night. He looked back. *Aptachuteh* lay behind him. The air here was warm and carried the breath of living things.

The mist was rising. Somewhere in the distance a bird sang. Alonqua turned his eyes from the dark place and looked ahead. His eyes grew wide with wonder at what he saw.

"I know that place, too," he whispered. "I know that Island. I know that it is shaped like the new moon. And I know the Great Tree which still grows upon the Island, white and gray. But I have not been here. I have never travelled across *Aptachuteh*. Did I see this place in a dream? Did my friend speak of it?"

The paddle moved swiftly, then slowed to a stroke that matched his breath. Alonqua began to hum a tune in a slow steady rhythm that kept pace, stroke by stroke, breath by breath. Single words joined the tune, isolated, disconnected—"Light...Sun... Moon...Sky...Child…"

Alonqua stilled the paddle, closed his eyes and drifted.

"Yes, I know now. I remember. My mother! Forgive my doubting mind. *Wanishi*—thank you—for the gift you sang to me so long ago when I was cradled in your arms. As you so often sang to me, I will sing to you. I ask *Manito* to carry my voice to the River of Stars."

Alonqua began with a whisper, but with each phrase his voice rose, and the melody and words were one. Never once did he take his eyes off the little island that floated before him like the dream of a long-lost world newly found.

Far, far away lies the Island of Light,
Beloved of the Sun,
Beloved of the Moon.
Go there my Child,
And grow in the Light.
On the Island of Light grows the Tree of Life,
Beloved of the Sky,
Beloved of the Earth.
Walk there my Child,
And rest in its shade.
In the Tree of Life, rests a Cradle of Wood,
Beloved of the Storm,

Beloved of the Rain,
Climb there my Child,
And heal in its arms."

And then there was only the silence of *Kitakima Telemaskek*, broken by the harsh call of a heron flying high over the water. Alonqua turned his eyes to the sun, just now rising above the ridgetop.

As the golden light spilled down the ridge and filled the valley, he made his way to the Island, the Island of Light. Like the sun it was old. Like the sun, the Island seemed newly risen, as if the words of a long-ago lullaby had brought it to life.

But before his canoe touched the Island, before he would walk there, Alonqua traveled the shoreline and found it to be the shape he recalled without having ever seen, that of *Weski Kishux*, the new moon. Halfway between the horns of the crescent rose a great tree. The trunk was broad and well-rooted, and its bark was a pearly white with patches of gray-brown, like the coat of a winter deer. Alonqua knew the tree to be of the family of *Xanikwe*, the ghost tree. The Whites called it sycamore.

Just before he left his canoe he looked closely at the tree.

"*Xanikwe*, your trunk is broad and strong, but it comes to its crown too soon. You should rise higher to touch the sky and gather the sun. Instead your many limbs stretch out far in all directions as your way to live and grow. We all do as we must. But what has happened to you, my friend?"

Alonqua turned his eyes to the Great Marsh. Removing moccasins, breechcloth and leggings, he waded out until the chill water reached his chin. He dove, rose, and dove once more to be certain no trace of *Aptachuteh* remained.

Here, clear and spring-fed, the living water received him. Dark threads of black decay rose from his body and were lost in *Kitakima's* gentle current. When he emerged, Alonqua touched his shoulder, chest, hair, and dove once more, rising only when he knew no trace of *Aptacuhteh* remained.

Once ashore he turned and reached out to the rising sun. When dry, he donned his breechcloth and leggings, leaving the moccasins on a log near the shore, and then turned to the tree. The great limbs cast shadows that stretched toward Alonqua, as if to draw him close. When he reached the great trunk he touched the smooth white bark. He turned and sat down, resting his back against *Xanikwe*, the old sycamore.

Alonqua slept until the sun touched his face and the morning had passed. He stretched and looked straight up through the branches to where the sun was riding high in a cloudless sky.

Rising to his feet, he saw the first limb was far too high to reach, and the smooth bark offered nothing to grip. Alonqua circled the tree for another way and found it. A large limb, still strong, broken loose through age and storm, had fallen and come to rest at the base of the sycamore. The upper end of the limb was still joined to the trunk, while the lower branches rested on the ground. The fallen limb was an easy climb. Once at the point where branch and tree met, he reached a higher limb and pulled himself up. From there the path upward was clear, and he climbed slowly, thoughtfully, limb by limb, to the place where the great tree ended and the sky began. On the way up pieces of old bark sloughed away, but where there should have been smooth, white, new bark beneath, Alonqua saw a dark, scar-like ridge rising all the way to the crown.

As he ran his hand along the scar, he whispered to the tree, "Beloved of the storm? How can this wound speak of love?"

Just above him the still-broad trunk disappeared within a nest of smaller branches. When Alonqua reached this tangle, he threaded his way through and broke free. And there was the place, nestled within the treetop, invisible to all who traveled below.

Alonqua closed his eyes and smiled. "In the Tree of Life rests a Cradle of Wood."

Eyes still closed, Alonqua ran his hands along the edge of the once-broken crown. The surface was smooth like skin and the bark, though blackened and hard as flint, showed no sign of decay.

Alonqua opened his eyes and looked to the sky.

"Great tree, I begin to see a little how you have grown

outward with your great arms, no longer upward, to touch the sun. The Thunder-Being chose you, loosed her spear, pierced you...broke you—and you have healed."

From the sky the boy's eyes moved down to the place beneath the smooth rim of the tree, and there rested a pool of water.

"Beloved of the Rain! Yes, my friend. Long ago the rain fell to cool your seared flesh, and now it has gathered here in your heart."

The trill of a frog rose from the shadowed place near the little pool. Alonqua bent his head toward the darkness and saw a wood-frog perched on a tiny ledge just above the water. Across the pool in faint sunlight a dusky spider waited for one of many hovering midges to find her web. Two water striders strummed the surface of their world. Just below the surface darted what could only be a minnow hatched from eggs brought by a bathing bird.

Alonqua reached his hand into the water, much warmer than that of the marsh, and when he could reach no deeper, held the hand still. The sun had risen to its highest point and much of the pool reflected the soft blue of a spring sky. And in the center of the little pool, looking back into his eyes were his own.

Only when the frog jumped and his face and the sky dissolved into rippling rings, did Alonqua retrieve his hand from the gift of the rain. He looked far out across the marsh to where he could just make out the dark, tangled maze of rotting trees.

"*Aptachuteh*, you are still there. I can see you. *Pamputis*, you still roam the edges of the dark waters. But I am here. My mother, my father, my friend are gone from the Earth, but they rest in my heart, just as I rest here."

Perhaps dark thoughts still troubled the corners of the boy's heart. Possibly thoughts of the White Man's bullets that took his father, and the White Man's sickness that stole his mother still lurked within.

But Alonqua rested in the heart of the Tree of Life, the Cradle of Wood, and for now he was beyond the reach of such things. And beyond *Aptachuteh* flowed the Sacred Springs, and at its heart were *Ahsen* and *Supkehelak* meeting in the Cradle of Stone. Near him lived *Xanhanni* the frog, *Xalaputis* the spider, and *Names* the little fish.

Just before Alonqua left the Cradle of Wood, before he climbed down limb by limb, he touched again the smooth bark which covered the wound, felt again the water of the little pool. And while his fingers moved through the still water, he felt life touch his hand and arm in a hundred different places.

"This is the secret," Alonqua whispered. "It is not only that this tree has healed, but that in the wound the tree has made a place for life—a small world full of life. The secret is that the tree has made its hurt a harbor of life."

Alonqua lifted water from the pool and touched the drops to his heart.

When in the golden light of the afternoon he returned to the canoe, he turned and thanked the ancient tree for revealing to his heart what his hurt had hidden.

CHAPTER 5
RESPECT

Alonqua did not linger on the island, much as that might have been tempting. The little food he had brought with him was nearly gone. The remaining strips of deer he chewed slowly; the ball of pemmican he saved. He gathered what little he had, his knife, his cape, rawhide packet, and nearly empty food satchel, and placed them in the canoe and pushed off. His lack of food was of little concern. Mawenteh said often the Great Marsh would provide if one knew its ways. And Alonqua knew them well.

He had traveled only a few strokes when he turned the canoe and looked back upon this place of wonder. From tip to tip the island measured no more than a hundred paces. Upon it he counted fifteen trees: six swamp maples, six willows, a chestnut tree, an ash tree, and *Xaxakwe*. Near *Xaxakwe* rose a low knoll, already bright green with early spring grass. Alonqua touched the medicine pouch beneath his buckskin top where lay the piece of bark.

"Were you the place at the end of my journey, I would be happy. But you are not. My Spirit Name awaits me, and I can have little rest until my true spirit and I find each other. *Wanishi*, Island of Light, Tree of Life, and the healing place at your heart. A part of you journeys with me. I will return here one day. I will climb and touch the little pool once more. And I will sleep on the green grass beneath the shade."

He turned the canoe to the east, and this time the dark water of *Aptachuteh* did nothing to slow his progress, found no foothold in his heart. For though he paddled slowly, carefully avoiding sunken logs and snags, his eyes were clear and untroubled, and he soon came to the farther edge, the lair of *Pamputis.* Soon after the sigh of falling water and the sheen of the Great Stone under the bright sun drew him near. But he paused only long enough to lower his head in reverence toward the sacred place, *Ahsen*, and *Supkehelak.*

"This journey began here," he whispered, "and here it will end."

And then Alonqua turned the canoe to the north, to a zone of vast reed islands, brown but tinged with the green of new growth. Choosing one of the channels that flowed strongest, he pushed on, soon reaching an open stretch of deeper water at the heart of the reeds. He pulled the paddle from the water and sniffed the air.

"So *Names,* you are here, just as I hoped. Your scent rises; you roam for food and I see your tracks move across the water." One of these tracks, broader and faster than the others, like a water spear, approached the canoe, disappeared then appeared on the other side. Alonqua felt his canoe wobble in the wake of the large fish.

"And," spoke Alonqua, "it seems one of you knows of me. So now we begin…"

Alonqua opened his rawhide bag and looked inside. Alongside the clam shells, flint, and tinder he found the fishbone hook and a coil of sinew thread. From the ball of pemmican in his food pouch he formed a smaller ball and embedded both barbs of the hook deep within. After uncoiling the string, he spun hook and bait a few times and sent them to the edge of the reeds. He twitched the line a few times, let out some slack, sat back and closed his eyes. The sun was still high, and Alonqua dozed a little in its warmth.

The line moved, the boy felt the twitch, opened his eyes and sat up.

"I feel you playing with the food, *Names,* but you are not yet ready. You will let me know when that time comes. I will not rush, not like the other time."

Alonqua gathered in the line, hand over hand, added a larger portion of pemmican and threw it back to the pool's edge.

"Have you heard of the other time—of my lesson, *Names*? I learned it here, two springs ago. It could be that you were my teacher. Even if you were, I would like to tell you what happened, if only to pass the time while you decide whether I have learned…"

A strange cry, like the call from a faraway world, drew his eyes to the sky. Three cranes, necks outstretched, were flying hard and fast.

"Did you hear them? Can you see them high above? The cranes are far-travelers. They swim in the river of wind that rises from the South. Soon their sharp beaks will probe mud for good things to eat, and they will fashion nests hidden in the reeds, and they will have young to teach their old ways."

The line twitched once more and then was still.

"Yes, *Names*, I stray from my story. It is good to speak of Spring. But I promised a story, and now if you will be still a moment I will tell it."

Alonqua pulled in the line once more, added more pemmican, and tossed it back.

"Now, if you were here at the time, you recall it was a day like this, only later in the spring. You will also recall I had already received several of your brothers and sisters, alive and fresh within the basket layered with soaked moss. I should have been grateful for that as a gift. But then I did not think of receiving. I thought of catching, of winning, of returning to the village with more fish than anyone. I wanted one more, and I foolishly asked *Manito* to make it be a big one!"

The boy smiled and shook his head.

"*Manito* heard me, but in a way I did not expect. The strike came from a great fish. I had never felt one stronger. The line cut my finger when I pulled against the power, and then it broke. But there it was—my end of the line floating on the water, just out of reach. Afraid it would disappear but still hopeful of the fish at the other end, I lunged for the line. This was very unwise! By the time I rose from the water and climbed into the canoe, I found that my basket full of fish was nowhere to be seen. I dove back in, retrieved the basket. Within it was a single clump of moss.

"My friends had a good laugh when I returned to the village and looked in my basket. They mocked me, called me 'Great Catcher of Fish' and wished to know my secret ways. Though they stung my pride, I did not defend myself with excuses. They were right to tease. I deserved it.

"Mawenteh told me many things, but it seems I had to live his lessons before I learned them. So it was with the empty basket. He had often said that *Manito* placed the animals upon the Earth as living gifts, and that I should love them, respect them, even as I hunt them to live. 'The deer, the fish, the crane that come in the spring—we are one!' I had heard his words, but now I felt the truth of them, and I was ashamed. I had played with the fish that day as if the Creator placed them in the water for some childish…"

Alonqua held his breath and leaned forward. He watched as the slack line played out and slowly disappeared beneath the water. He looked at his hand, saw the scar, and quickly tied his end of the line to the center of the paddle. The line tautened; he placed both hands on the paddle and pulled back hard. At the setting of the hook the water exploded as the great fish rose, shaking head and tail in fury. Alonqua held on as the huge pike dove, rose again, doubled back in an attempt to dislodge the hook. The water churned and foamed, but both line and hook held firm. Then as quickly as it had begun, the battle ceased. The line, still taut, pivoted, and the canoe moved with the great fish, slowly, steadily, through the reeds.

Soon the fish surfaced, and Alonqua saw what he had known from the first strike. This truly was a great fish, nearly as long as he was tall. Even after the hard fight he swam with strong heavy fin-strokes, pulling both boy and canoe through reed channels toward some distant destination.

Alonqua leaned forward and spoke softly.

"If I did not need all of this line for the journey to come, I would cut it and release you despite my hunger. You are proud and strong, and I do not think it is the line that holds you. Were it your wish you would have the strength to release yourself."

The canoe moved more slowly; the fin strokes grew feeble. Alonqua looked up to see that the fish had nearly reached the shore and was turning toward a narrow channel. The entrance was nearly hidden by a tangle of willow branches. Before the great fish turned to enter, Alonqua released the line from the paddle and tied it to his leg. There was just enough room for him to turn the canoe and follow. The channel was straight, deep and free of snags; the roof of the willow tunnel forced Alonqua to lie back in the canoe. He watched the cloudless afternoon sky through the moving maze of willow wands, and felt the constant pull on his leg where he had tied the line.

Soon the branches thinned out, and then there was only the sky. Alonqua sat up to see the canoe was in the center of a small pool in the heart of the willows. The canoe was still, and the fish lay motionless, body turned to the side; only the gill still moved, rising up and down with the rhythm of a human breath.

Alonqua untied the string and drifted to the side of the fish. Under the late afternoon sun the scales shimmered in bands of green and gold, but even now the colors were fading. He saw the eyes, still fierce and wild, darken and cloud with evening mist.

"Is this where you were born? Have you returned to your first home?"

The boy reached to his side and released the sharp blade. His voice was very soft, almost a whisper.

"You are very old. You have fought many battles. I understand why you brought me here, to your first home."

He stroked the smooth flank of the great fish until he found the place. A quick thrust, a quiver of flesh and the blood flowed fast, tinging the water in crimson threads. The gills rose once, twice, once again, trembled and closed. The eyes held no light.

"You chose, *Names*. You knew it was time. And now your spirit swims once more in the River of Stars."

Already the flow of blood had ceased, and the long body of the great fish began to settle deeper into the pool. Alonqua coiled the slack line round his leg and pulled the fish alongside. Together they reached the edge of the pool where the ground was firm. The willows were few there, and soft moss grew thick. Alonqua grounded the canoe, climbed out and onto the shore, pulling the fish with him. He knelt and placed his hand on the wound, where there remained a trace of blood.

He remained silent a long time. Then he raised his head and reached for the knife. There was work to do, and the gift must not be squandered.

"*Wanishi, Names*, for this gift, for the honor of your trust in me, that you chose me to release you from a body that was old and tired. But please know, that old as you were, tired as you were, I have never known such a strong fight! The flesh you have left behind will strengthen me for my journey. The strength of your spirit remains in my heart. *Wanishi, Manito*—that you find me worthy of this gift."

The sun was perched upon the western ridge and the air was cooling. This was a good place to rest and eat. A little creek flowed into the marsh only a few paces away. There was plenty of dry firewood scattered about. A downed willow provided chips left behind by *Temakwe*, the beaver, perfect for smoking fish. This time he had no ember, but he had flint, knife, and tinder, and soon there was a glow, then a tiny flame, then a fire. In the last light of day Alonqua scrubbed the fish with reeds soaked in clear water until the skin as free of scales. After cutting the fish into large chunks and narrow strips he cut away pieces of the upper spine as Mawenteh had taught him. He found the pair of ear-stones embedded just behind each eye. One he left in place; the other he removed and carried to the water. The blood washed away, the ear-stone lay shimmering in his hand, pearly white in the evening light.

"*Names*, you have granted me the gift of your body. I will receive of it all I can. This stone I will keep with me through all of my life. I will place this deep in my medicine pouch. The stone will touch the flake of bark from the Tree of Life. Someday, if it is your wish, you might speak to me from The River of Stars. I leave the other stone with your body so that you might have it. When I am lonely and the stars are hidden and cannot hear, I will call your name. Perhaps you will hear me, and we will speak to one another."

The late afternoon breeze had died away, and the marsh lay silent and golden in the fading light. Night was coming on and Alonqua had only a little time to gather more firewood and enough green sticks to build a smoking platform. He drove four long forked sticks deep in the ground two paces apart around the fire, placed two long sticks in the notches then the rest of the sticks across, a hand's width apart. Upon these he placed the strips of fish. By morning they would be smoked and dried, more than enough to fill his pouch. The chunks of fish he wrapped in the skin and set upon the coals at the fire's edge. While the skin browned and crackled, he gathered fresh watercress from the stream.

Alonqua knelt by the fire, fed it with a few more sticks, and turned the cold side of the roasting fish toward the core of the fire. Then from the marsh rose the faint sound of little splashes and squeals. Rising from the fire, he followed the channel until he reached the reeds just short of the open water. The splashes and tiny voices were close, and Alonqua crept close to see who was there.

"Ah, *Kwenoomuk*!" he whispered in delight, "and your young ones! For a moment I thought children of my village had followed me here just to tease me on my great journey! I am very glad it is you!"

The marsh held just enough light to reveal four swimmers, one large, three smaller, weaving silver lines across the still water. The otter family had come to feed, but, as is their way, to play as well. Alonqua moved yet closer as the mother otter rose from the water holding a wriggling fish. Nearby three little heads also rose, their voices like babies' laughter as they awaited the prize.

With a flick of her muzzle the fish rose, fell, and disappeared in a boil of water and spray. While one swam away to enjoy the prize, the mother caught another and tossed it up. When all three children had their fill, she led her young along the marsh edge. Alonqua watched as they dove beneath and glided over floating logs. Upon one log she paused long enough for the little ones to join her. They were just yearlings, still a season away from being on their own. Here, in turn, she stroked the sleek fur of each one, and each one she nuzzled until their little voices, softer now, rose once again. Her voice, still child-like, but lower, joined theirs. Then they were gone.

The sun, just as silently, departed the sky. Alonqua stood and looked back to his hidden place through the trees. The firelight drew him to a warm meal, a gift touched by fire, and to rest.

When he had finished eating and taken a long drink, he placed more wood upon the fire and once again the mist rose, enfolding the marsh in its gentle arms. Alonqua knelt before the fire and spoke softly.

"*Manito*, you who breathe life into stars and young otters, *Wanishi*, for this day of gifts…My body is full. My heart is full...I have warmth...I have life. And I have the promise of a new day. May my actions be worthy of this promise."

He lay back, closed his eyes, crossed his hands on his chest, and smiled to feel the slow steady beat of a heart on the right path. Soon he slept, and his hands remained upon his heart till the night grew old, and day paused at the threshold.

~~~

A heavy sound, like a great stone hurled into the water, pierced Alonqua's sleep like a spear of ice. As he scrambled to his feet the echoes of the impact faded, only to be followed by the sound of waves lapping the shore. A great wind, sudden and powerful, tore at the fire, driving showers of sparks into the darkness. Alonqua lurched away from the fire and looked toward the marsh. Even from this distance he heard it, something vast and powerful—old, old as the Earth, was moving from the water to the land.

If within him there was a voice that called him to run, Alonqua had no ears for it. Beneath an ancient oak, branches writhing in the wind, he stood, arms at his side, breathless, eyes searching the dark. The wind died all at once as if in mid-breath. The air grew heavy and reeked of wet earth, the dens of animals, the nests of birds, of decay and rot, of spring and life.

A shadow darker than the darkest night rose up before him, and Alonqua reached out to the old oak and held on.

"*Mesingw!*" Alonqua whispered in wonder, "why have you come here—to me?"
~~~

CHAPTER 6
TRUST

The shadow did not reply, nor did it take form, but, risen from the marsh, *Mesingw,* the Ancient Guardian, had come for Alonqua. A rivulet of darkness flowed from the shadow and touched the boy softly just above his heart. Though just a gentle brush, such was the power of *Mesingw* that the boy lurched away in pain, striking the trunk of the old oak, then sinking to his knees.

Through the hurt, he looked again to the shadow, now like a great bear rising on its hind legs to sniff the wind. And then appeared the eyes, a pair of faint pale moons, and below the eyes there was the vague notion of a torso, arms and legs. When *Mesingw* turned his eyes from Alonqua and began to move through the forest, what the boy saw was not the shambling gait of *Maxkwa*, the bear, but the slow graceful pace of an old and honored chief leading his tribe to battle.

And Alonqua followed, though even had he the power to speak, he likely could not say why. The journey, now at the gates of dawn, first angled away from the marsh through dense forest, then back to the water. As he moved through the forest the day was coming on in slow waves, and the soft-gray light, seeping down through tangled branches, gathered in little pools. Alonqua did not see these pools of light reach out, join other pools, nor hear the songs of the awakening birds, nor smell the scent of dawn. *Mesingw* now moved swiftly. Already his shape was melting away in the growing light. Alonqua's eyes strayed nowhere else. Breathing hard, he struggled to keep pace over logs and through tangles. And always there was the engulfing smell of death and life, of rot and new growth.

Just as Alonqua emerged from the forest and drew near the marsh, the water exploded in a fountain of spray. As he had come from the water, so had *Mesingw* returned. His guide was gone, leaving Alonqua at a place he knew well. At his side flowed the channel that had ushered him to the marsh on the night of rain. And out across a narrow stretch of water, half-hidden in the mist, rose the lodge of *Temakwe*. Alonqua, still breathing hard, arms and face scratched and bleeding, watched the ripples of water touch the shore.

Alonqua looked back in the direction of his camp, his canoe, his food. But if thoughts of returning entered his mind, they were cut short by the sound, one unlike any he had known. The high rasping snarl held both pain and rage, and the source was close.

Alonqua froze. This was not a sound that beckoned approach, but chilled one's very heart. Even so, he did not turn away, but ran up the channel toward the river, jumped a feeder spring and came to a little tree. When the cry, so close now, rose again, he looked up to see a small tree shake and bend. And there, just on the other side of the tree, Alonqua saw her.

Eyes glittering, she glared back at the boy, and for just a moment she and the tree were still.

The otter was breathing hard and fast, bits of foam near her mouth and scattered on her coat.

"*Kwenoomuk,*" Alonqua breathed. He approached her and knelt close by—too close. Her lunge was swift and savage, her teeth nearly reaching his hand. Backing away a little, he spoke softly to her.

"I have no wish to hurt you, *Kwenoomuk.* I fear you are already hurt, and I wish only to help you. If you do not trust, if you fight me, I fear you will die."

The morning light was not yet strong, but Alonqua was close enough to see the braided wire cutting into the otter's belly and trailing up to a thin strong branch. Scattered around her was a circle of torn leaves and clawed earth, and upon these were drops and smears of blood, some dry, some fresh. There was no telling just how long she had struggled.

Alonqua leaned toward her as far as he dared.

"*Kwenoomuk*, what can we do?"

The otter answered with another snarl, her eyes locked on his.

"I had—I have—a friend, old, kind, very wise. He knew the *Kwenoomuk* well, that your tribe is fierce and proud, that even a wolf or bear will not fight you, that you are no camp dog eager for a human touch. I learned from my friend that one so full of pain as you sees my hand as a foe, though it seeks to free you. I would be slow with you, but there is little time. The wire is deep. Another struggle might kill you. The trapper must be close, and if the wire does not take your life, this man surely will. I know him. He is never alone. He and the others know of me. I find their snares and traps and I throw them in the marsh. I hide the dead deep in the forest. *Kwenoomuk*, these men are white and I have ruined their trapping. If they find me here we will both die.

Alonqua edged closer, then pulled away once more as the otter coiled for another strike.

"Do you know, *Kwenoomuk*, that it was *Mesingw* who heard your cries, watched your struggles?

"I know he is the Guardian for you and your animal brothers, that he is old as the Earth and has great power. But *Mesingw* came to me. He has no hand of flesh to loosen the wire. A human hand set the trap. A human hand must free you. This hand—my hand—which I offer now."

The hand, moving ever-so-slowly toward the otter was received with raking claws and snapping teeth.

"*Kwenoomuk*, how can I carry my words through your pain and into your heart? How?"

As Alonqua spoke these words, the otter, just for an instant turned her eyes to a patch of reeds just offshore. Only then did he hear them call out to her.

"Your children! Are you the family I watched playing in the marsh? Three little ones, born last spring. *Kwenoomuk*, they are young. They catch the fish you offer, but they are still learning. I know you have taught them to be silent when apart from you. Until now. They hear your pain, and they are afraid. And now they cry out, and you fight to be near them. But you cannot fight this wire."

Alonqua sat back and crossed his arms. The early morning wind flowed over the marsh, bending the reeds and ruffling the water. The otter looked again toward her children, then back to Alonqua, regarding the boy through a haze of pain. And so they watched each other and waited. Again, Alonqua reached out his hand, nearly touching her flank, but this time she did not miss. Only one of her claws found its mark, but it dug deep.

Alonqua cradled his bleeding hand with the other as he pulled away.

"Your children, *Kweenoomuk*! If I cannot speak for them...if their cries only move you to fight, I can do nothing."

Alonqua released his wounded hand and watched the trickle of blood drip to the earth. His eyes filled with tears and he cried out.

"Hear me! My mother held this hand all the night before she left me. She lay in the snare of her fever. I call for my mother every night. This hand could not save her! This hand can free you. You have only to lie still! Help me help you! For your children who need you...for my mother…"

His voice trailed off. Kneeling before her, hands clasped, eyes closed, Alonqua did the only thing he knew to do. He sang.

"Far, far away lies the Island of Light,
Beloved of the Sun,
Beloved of the Moon,
Go there, dear Mother
And live in the Light."

At first, Alonqua could not hear his own voice, but as each phrase grew louder, the otter swung her head and fixed her eyes on the boy.

"On the Island of Light grows the Tree of Life,
Beloved of the Earth,
Beloved of the Sky,
Lie there, dear Mother,

And rest in its shade.
"In the Tree of Life rests a Harbor of Wood,
Beloved of the Storm,
Beloved of the Rain,
Sleep there, dear Mother
And heal in her arms."

When the last word was taken up by the rising wind, Alonqua opened his eyes to see the eyes of otter soften, then slowly close. Her rigid body, so weary of the pain, uncoiled, and her breathing, so ragged, grew deep and calm.

It was time.

Alonqua reached out to her, touched her damp sleek fur with his wounded hand, and held it there, near her heart. He felt her chest rise and fall, her strong muscles still twitching with the memory of her pain.

"*Wanishi, Kwenoomuk.* Your trust is a great gift to grant me this touch. I will repay your gift with mine."

Placing a hand on either flank he gently drew her to the tree which held the wire. The tension eased, the otter opened her eyes and looked toward her children still hidden in the reeds.

"Not yet, *Kwenoomuk.* Lie still."

Placing one hand on her heart, his other searched her belly. When he found the wire he traced it to the binding place and tried to feed it through. The wire, tightly cinched and still embedded in her flesh, failed to loosen. She flinched with pain, reopening the wound, bathing the wire with fresh blood.

Her blood, slippery like oil, and Alonqua's steady hand, joined to unlock the snare and loosen enough to ease the wire free of the wound. She remained still as he slid the loop from her body.

The otter rose, fell, and rose once more. She took a few steps from the boy and paused as if waiting for the agony of a tightening wire. A few more steps and she knew she was free.

She bolted to the water and entered with the smoothness of a drop of rain. The otter was hurt, but she was strong, and she would find her children, and she would heal. He stood on the shore and tried to see the journey home, but the swift arrow of her wake was soon lost in the reeds.

Alonqua's final gift to her was a chant, a simple song often sung by his old friend as they walked the woods. Mawenteh called it a morning song, a song of new life, new journeys. The chant held but one word, "*Kishelamukong,*" the One who created the Earth and Stars. As the sun rose above the ridge, and the light spilled across the valley, Alonqua sang the song, the melody and the word rising and falling like the waves of a distant sea.

Kishelamukong .... Kishelamukong ...
A-weh, a-weh, a-weh...
A-weh, a-weh, a-weh...
Kishelamukong.... Kishelamukong...

A commotion from the reed island told the story of reunion and brought the song to a close. There was but one thing left to do. Reaching down for the snare and finding a heavy stick, Alonqua wrapped the wire tightly around it and flung both far out into the marsh.

He stared at his hand, then lifted the other and held them side by side. Upon one was the blood of *Kwenoomuk*; upon the other, his own. He looked again to the reed island where the children, even now, greeted their mother in a wriggling swarm. He lowered his head in the direction of the mother, clasped his hands, then knelt and bathed them in the cool water. The blood joined in little swirls and disappeared.

A clam shell like the one that held the ember lay upon a piece of wood near the water's edge. Alonqua reached down, lifted the shell to his eyes and saw the toothmarks of an otter still etched on the rim where it was pried open. The inner shell glowed like a gossamer rainbow. He placed the gift beneath his tunic and turned toward the channel to begin the journey back to his camp.

"Josh, over here! I see tracks!"

The shout was close, near the water's edge, just through the trees. Alonqua froze only an instant, then bolted toward the channel, his only chance. He came to a log spanning the water, made it halfway across, and noiselessly slipped into the water.

Now Alonqua was in the snare, and the wire was closing fast.

CHAPTER 7
HAVEN

Chest-deep water still held the chill of winter. Alonqua plunged to the bottom and fought to pull himself along the snag-filled channel. His only chance was to hold his breath and hug the bank, stay out of sight until he reached the bend in the channel where winter ice and spring rains carve out cavities beneath the bank. Lungs burning, he reached such an undercut just as his pursuers closed in. Raising his head through a web of tangled roots, he sucked in quick breath from the narrow gap between water and earth. The ground above him sagged as one of his pursuers stood on the bank just above him.

"Watch it, Josh, this dirt ain't none too firm!"

"Serve ya right, Simon, if ya fell in, losin' him that way."

As the first man stepped back, the earth rose, and Alonqua released a slow silent breath.

"Ain't lost him yet, by Gawd. I swear I saw him back by that holler tree lyin' 'cross the water. Musta jumped in, an' by Gawd, I ain't seen him climb out. All we do now is wait 'im out. Reckon we got 'im! We got our man."

Trying to still his ragged breath and shivering body, Alonqua looked downstream through the slice of light and saw that the sheltering undercut extended toward the marsh and disappeared at a bend in the channel. His back hugging the cold mud, he edged his way, half-step by half-step, aware that even a ripple would catch watchful eyes. But the bend was drawing nearer; once around that there was the marsh.

But just as Alonqua reached the curve of the channel he felt a solid mass of tangled roots in his path. There was no way through, under or over it, only around, forcing him out in open water. He could have lunged out and around, and just at that moment the men's eyes might be elsewhere. But Alonqua knew these men, that they were well-skilled in the ways of his own people even as they hunted them. They were the trackers. They were patient and their eyes and ears missed nothing. But his body was giving out as the cold water took its toll. To remain where he was until the watchers left would mean death, his body to remain here, unclaimed, his bones picked clean by *Pamputis*.

He drew in a long deep breath. It had to be now. Willing himself into the open channel, Alonqua glanced toward the men only a stone's throw upstream. Just as he reached the tip of the root, before he could twist around it, one of the men turned.

Eyes: level, cold, and hard, locked on his, and the man's mouth tightened to a scowl. The moment hung there, frozen like a spear of ice in a cave of stone. Nothing moved. Not the water, the air, nor Alonqua's heart, his breath, nor the eyes of the man and boy. And then a shadow flowed across the channel, and both pairs of eyes followed it until they looked up to see the lone eagle soar across the marsh and disappear into the fire of the rising sun.

"*Wanishi, Opalanie,*" the boy whispered. "If you are the last of what I see on this Earth, I am thankful."

Alonqua turned to face the man with the gun. Chest-deep in the cold water, the boy drew in a long, slow breath, and awaited the bullet which must surely come. And then he saw the man's iron eyes melt, the scowl uncoil. And the boy watched him turn away and heard him speak angry words to his partner across the channel.

"Si, you're so all-fired sure you saw him jump in, so where is he? Seems to me if you saw right we'd have him by now!"

"I tell ya, Joshua, I saw him. Mornin' sun was in my eyes, mebbe, but I saw somethin' big slide intuh that water, and he's gotta come out!"

"Show me where. There oughta be tracks."

The moment the man called Josh pointed up the channel, Alonqua took his chance. He lunged around the root, dove deep like an otter, swam past the bend and out into the cold hands of the *Kitakima Telamaskek*. When at last he rose for a quick breath, just ahead was the mound of sticks and logs, the lodge of *Temakwe*.

Again he dove, and swam near the bottom through a maze of arrowroot newly risen from the mud. Just a few body lengths from the lodge he rose to the surface, gasped in a breath and disappeared. He reached out his hands and grasped one stick, then another, until he had pulled himself to the far side. Sheltered from the shore he paused to take in several deep breaths, then dove for the opening.

His fingers were numb, but still he wrapped them around thick branches to pull himself to the base. He had nearly circled the lodge when his hand reached out for another stick and felt nothing but a narrow span of open water. He rose to chance a single breath and to place his medicine pouch in a niche between sticks, then dove to the opening. There Alonqua turned his body, thrust forward his arms, and pulled his head through the gap. Too narrow. He released his lungful of air, found a firm handhold and pulled again. Breechcloth, leggings, and buckskin top, held fast by the sharpened sticks, tore away. Elbows now wedged against the sides of the passage, he squirmed to move them forward, but the more he struggled, the more the passage tightened around him like a wooden snare. His lungs burned for air; his body was spent. His mouth formed silent words in the cold darkness.

"Here I will die."

The last bubbles rose from his mouth. He turned his head and saw them rise so slowly, sifting through the weave of wood.

A violent push and searing pain.

An upward surge.

Darkness…

Stillness…

A gasp for breath...another...then another…

The touch of earth beneath his hand...the smell of marsh grass and willow…

He opened his eyes and turned on his back. He opened his mouth, only to feel his hand stifle the cry of pain. He moved his hand to his heart, felt the drumbeat grow steady and slow. And when he knew he was alive the boy slowly sat up, and whispered one word…

"Mesingw!"

His breechcloth and buckskin top were gone, ripped away. He felt for his medicine pouch—gone, no, not gone, saved. He reached out to either side and found himself upon a thin bed of dry grass and soft willow bark. Grabbing handfuls of each, Alonqua rubbed his body until warmth returned. But with the warmth came more pain and the flow of blood from deep gouges on his chest and arms. He lay back and closed his eyes, breathing slow and deep, until the pain ebbed to a distant throb.

At last he sat up and opened his eyes to see the darkness softened by a faint shimmer. Above him, at the peak of the lodge a loosely woven tangle of sticks ushered in a trace of sun. Alonqua found he was sitting on a hard dirt platform upon which the beaver had placed tufts of sweet grass and willow chips. This platform tilted up to another smaller terrace just under the roof. On both sides lay piles of fresh spring willow shoots.

The lodge basked under a high sun, and after the chill water, the warmth was life-giving. Sudden voices told another story. The men were close, possibly already at the edge of the marsh searching the surface. Alonqua knew the language, but the words were muffled by the distance and the thick weave of sticks and mud. One voice bristled with anger; the other responded with impatience. Again, the boy tasted fear. But as the moments stretched out, he breathed easier. There were no tracks to follow, and the marsh revealed no secrets, only the water, the trees, the reeds, and a lone island of wood.

The voices settled into low murmurs, and the boy uncoiled a little, even stretched out and closed his eyes. There was silence as the boy, weak and tired, drifted in the shallows of sleep.

"Simon, let's clear out!"

Alonqua sat up, too dazed to understand. Crawling to the side, he placed his ear against the mud wall.

"Even if you saw what you thought saw, he's gone. We're wastin' time. Let's go!"

"Don't need to yell, Josh, I'm right beside ya. Anybody'd hear ya a mile away. I know yer mad, but I tell ya he's got to be right around here!"

"I'm through waitin'. I'm goin.' If I leave now I'll get back 'fore sundown. You like travelin' in the dark, stay for all I care! Caused enough trouble seein' things!"

"Dammit, Joshua, I saw what I saw! He's got to be close...it's as if the swamp swallered him whole!"

"All right, I've had enough. Simon, let's go! Now!"

Alonqua lay back and released a long, slow breath. The *Temakwe,* he knew, were close by, and they must be longing to return to their home for food and rest. The boy turned on his side and whispered to them.

"A little while more and I will be gone. You understand well the dangers of the day, and I know you grant me these moments until the light fades and I can move with the night. I ask this of you, your wife, your little ones. And because I am weak, and must travel to my camp, I ask one gift more—something—my friend."

The faint column of light sifting through the lodge-top angled down and came to rest upon a little stack of green willow wands. Alonqua reached out, picked one up, peeled away the thin bark, and pulled the stick through clenched teeth. The thin soft inner layer, sweet like spring, bitter like winter, held life. His teeth stripped the food from three more sticks, then he lay back to settle his stomach.

He was tired but he did not sleep. Instead he watched the faint sliver of light move from the pile of willow to the wall, the wall to the higher terrace, all the while taking on the orange and red of evening. When the last trace of light was lost, he heard stirrings in the water near the lodge. Night had fallen on the marsh. *Temakwe* the beaver had returned. And now it was time to find his way.

There was the matter of the underwater passage, but when he reached down into the little pool, Alonqua smiled at what he found. It was *Temakwe's* way. Were the dam to break and the entrance become exposed the invader, a wolf or fisher, would be snagged in a gauntlet of sharpened sticks. Moving out of the lodge would prove different than the boy's entrance. With no clothes to catch, and the branches curving away from him, the passage would still be tight, but also smooth. This time he needed no help. Before entering the water he lifted a tuft of sweet grass from the *Temakwe*'s bed and held it tight against his heart.

"*Wanishi*, my friends, for this little gift. Someday, I will twine and burn this, and direct the sacred smoke to protect your family, as your home has protected me."

On his way through the passage he retrieved the torn buckskin top, then his leggings. He rose and surfaced and found the medicine pouch. A wake of silver ripples followed him as he swam for the shore. Emerging from the marsh he turned and looked back to the lodge, now melting away in the evening mist.

"Just now you are returning," he whispered. "I have left your home as I have found it, save a few sticks. For this haven, for this food. *Wanishi*, my brothers. We both will have stories to tell about this day. My friend, Mawenteh, spoke of the *Temakwe* as an ancient and honored tribe. He said you of all the tribes best understand the need for a place safe from harm. I give thanks for what my friend called *welesewaken*, your kindness…but the trappers will return. May you shun their traps."

Alonqua walked slowly to the place of pain and struggle and release. Scattered about were the tattered leaves, the torn earth, and the dry blood of *Kwenoomuk.* Opening his medicine pouch he reached for the shell and held it under the moon. Her soft light filled the cup and spilled over onto his cold hand. He returned the gift to the pouch, along with the sweet grass of *Temakwe's* lodge, retied the cord, and placed them under his torn tunic.

He looked up to the Sun of the Night. From the bright crescent of a few nights ago, she now waxed brighter, now halfway on her journey to become the Full Frog Moon.

"I am thankful you travel with me, *Pishkeweni Kishux*. I am cold. But I have your light to show me the way to my camp. They have given up the chase for the night. And I will eat, and I will sleep beside the fire."

Beneath the soft light, the boy clothed himself and turned to the dark path which brought him to this place.

"*Mesingw*," he whispered. "Are you here? For the two lives you spared today, *Wanishi*, old spirit. *Kwenoomuk* is with her young. I have my life. We will not forget."

The boy glanced to the moon, breathed deep, once, twice, then turned from the marsh and melted into the arms of the moon-shadowed forest.

CHAPTER 8

SIKON TALEKA

The journey back to his camp was hard. What he found when he came to the clearing was far harder. His canoe had been dragged from the water's edge and lay alongside the dead fire. Two jagged holes hacked in the bottom stared back at the boy until he turned away and staggered to a nearby tree. He reached up to a strong limb and held on.

The moon was sliding down the sky, and soon it would touch the western ridge. But when Alonqua at last let go of the branch and looked back, the faint light revealed all. There was the boat, now useless to him. The paddle was unbroken, thrust blade-first into the soft earth. And the food bag hung from the paddle, empty.

Alonqua felt for the medicine pouch beneath his buckskin top. It was all he had left.

The boy turned to the marsh and watched the mirrored moon float upon the stillness. Reaching down to pick up a stone he hurled it far out, and one moon shattered. To the Sky Moon, the whole one, Alonqua lifted his eyes and spoke.

"*Pishkeweni Kishux*, I speak to you. I would speak to my friend, but I do not know where he has gone. If he were near, Mawenteh, the heart-gatherer, would surely help me gather mine. Do you see the canoe? My friend and I chose the tree, and I helped him hollow the log, and smooth the sides. I was very young, but Mawenteh praised my work. The canoe was ours, and together we traveled the river and marsh."

Alonqua pointed to the broken shell of wood.

"Do you see? I have escaped from death, but still the White Man finds a way to wound me. I will find food. My friend taught me well. But the fish gave its life to me. And they have taken it. They left the paddle and the empty bag for me to see. They mock me!"

Alonqua's fist unclenched and like sunlight upon snow, a faint smile rose from his heart. Placing one hand on the ruined canoe, Alonqua opened his medicine pouch with the other. With the sharp edge of the clamshell gift he carved away a finger-sized piece of the craft that had carried him this far. Once these were secured in the bag, he found his words.

"No, *Piskeweni Kishux*, not all. No! Not all of them. I did not escape. I was set free. Someday I will return this gift. But now, before the dawn, I must eat and find a place to rest. I cannot stay here."

He recalled the nearby spring and there he knelt, cupped his hands, drew the water to his lips and drank. The water entered him; its spirit traveled the channels of his body, and touched his heart. Within an arm's reach a gathering of watercress had risen from the spring-water, and he gladly accepted a portion of this gift, chewing slowly, savoring each tender leaf and stem.

It was a start.

Alonqua leaned back and watched the moon.

"Soon you will leave the sky and darkness will hide the forest trails until the sun rises. I will follow you to the West, and when your light no longer guides me I will stop there and rest. So, lead on. My friend, Mawenteh, follows his own path and cannot help me. *Pishkeweni Kishux,* you must be my guide. I have no other."

So Alonqua left the broken camp and entered the forest. His eyes stayed fixed on the half-moon, while his silent feet felt their way. Not a sound—not from his steps, nor his breath. The trees spoke to him soundless words, and the animals of the night watched him as he passed. At last the moon touched the treetops of the distant ridge; she dimmed, and then was gone.

When the last silver glow faded from the western sky, Alonqua stopped and looked up at the stars. And then he heard them. And he smiled.

When one beacon fades, there will be another. It was not the stars he heard, but a beacon of voices, first one, then another, then many, silver voices like singing stars.

"Yes!" whispered Alonqua. "I hear you! And I know the place. Mawenteh and I were there only last spring. Now you sing again."

The beckoning voices rose and fell in gentle waves and drew him at last to the place he knew well. The pool nestled in the sheltered nook like water held by cupped hands. No spring fed this pool. The rain and snowmelt gathered here, and the water warmed in the spring sun. By summer the pool would be dry, but by then the seeds of the spring singers would have sprouted.

And next spring they would gather at the pool with new songs. But just now, all at once, the singing ceased and the pool lay empty and silent.

"No need to stop, my friends, just because I am here. I have been listening for you all through my journey, *Sikon Taleka.* In the hollow place in the Tree of Life, I heard your brother. I must say he was first to sing. But his pool was small, high in a tree, open to the sun. And his voice was small and would not be heard unless one was close. Not you, you are many, and you sing to other forest pools where even now others of your tribe hear you and open their eyes."

To grant the little ones space, Alonqua withdrew from the pool and climbed the low ridge which sheltered three sides. On top he found a carpet of spring moss and there he sat, perched above the water. Then one call, another and another, and once more the little hollow rang with song. Alonqua reached into his medicine pouch and retrieved a little pouch holding a shard of flint, a piece of steel and bits of dried lichen.

Some dry leaves and twigs, a spark, and the little flame was soon a warming fire. A few larger branches and his island of light grew to include a chestnut tree. Some of the nuts, still nestled in spiny husks, lay scattered around the tree. Wary of the spines,

Alonqua husked and gathered a few handfuls and placed them in the coals to roast.

"This is a good place," he said to the little ones lining the water's edge, "which you know far better than I. But before I sleep, I wish to tell you a goodnight story. I smile because this story is more for me than you. But even if the story is for me, it is about you. You know it, but maybe you would like to hear it. My friend, Mawenteh, told me this story the spring after my mother died, on a night like this, and you were singing, just as you are now. I will try to recall his words."

And one by one the little frogs grew silent, until only a few called, back and forth, across the pool.

Alonqua reached for a stick and rolled the chestnuts from the coals. He picked one up, tossed it from hand to hand until it was cool enough to peel. Tossing away the shell he chewed slowly, savoring the warm sweet meat.

"That's better. More are waiting, but so are you." He leaned toward the pool below, cleared his throat, and began.

"This is an old story, *Sikon Taleka*, from the time of Turtle Island, just after the Creator formed the Earth and all that walks, swims, or flies. It is the story of how your tribe was chosen to chase away the snows of winter and proclaim the birth of spring. You likely know *Manito's* first choice was *maxkwa,* the bear, because he was the largest, and strongest of all the animal tribes. And when he rose on two legs his roar shook the forest. *Manito* instructed *maxwa* that he must release his roar at the moment the sun joined the winds of the South. *Maxwa*, so proud of this honor that he strutted a little, spoke to *Manito.*

"Great Spirit, you have chosen well. Not only am I the strongest and smartest, I make the most noise!"

Alonqua reached for another chestnut, peeled it and chewed slowly.

"I ask your pardon, *Sikon Taleka,* but I am very hungry and do not wish the sounds of my empty stomach to drown out my words! But now the story. You recall that the bear was well-prepared to perform the task. At least the bear thought so. But you must recall what happened. The great and mighty *maxkwa* was so lazy from a long winter nap he slept through the day of sun and warm wind. With no one to call out her coming, Spring refused to arrive. Harsh winter had her way and lay heavy and cold on the barren land.

"*Manito* was very angry at Bear and his words rolled out like thunder, 'A whole year lost! No Spring! No Summer! No Autumn! Only Winter! If you, *Maxkwa*, the largest, is unfit for the task, I will choose the smallest! And *Maxkwa,* that long bushy tail of which you are so proud? Look now!'

"And Bear looked around and down. His tail, once long and full, was now reduced to a little stubby tuft of hair, which, try as he might, he could not tuck between his legs as he crept away."

Manito turned from the fleeing bear and spoke once more, 'I choose now the tribe of little ones who will feel the sun and warm winds as they awaken in sheltered forest pools. From these sacred places they will sing out to all that Spring has come to the land. So that all will hear, I will give the little frogs a big voice. And will also bestow upon this tribe a name, *Sikon Taleka*. He Who Sings Spring to Life!"

His ate his last chestnut and when it was gone, Alonqua cleared his throat and resumed.

"And had not the other animals been afraid of *Manito's* anger, they would have laughed at this choice. They thought you small and weak, but as the years flowed by, spring after spring you proved them wrong. Winter would fight back, cover your pools with ice, but you looked up through the ice and knew the South winds would return, and you would at last silence the cold winds with your call of life."

Alonqua yawned and stretched, then reached out his hand to test the softness of the moss.

"*Wanishi, Sikon Taleka*. I had need to tell the story even if you had no need to hear it. It is a good story. And now I need rest. I feel, little ones, a great day awaits me. I do not wish to be the lazy bear who fails to rise to his mission."

Perhaps sensing the story was done, the frogs, one by one, joined their songs until the little hollow rang with new life. Alonqua lay down upon the soft spring moss and turned to his side so that he could look upon the shimmering stars tossed upon the water.

Alonqua closed his eyes, and if his mind turned to *Kwenoomuk,* to the trappers, or to his mother, or to Mawenteh, it is likely no thought lingered. He was tired, and the *sikon taleka* lifted their voices to the stars and sang him to sleep.

CHAPTER 9
STORM

Alonqua awakened at dawn to a rising wind. He sat up from his moss bed, turned his face to the South, and felt the heavy push of this strange morning air. The unsheltered trees high on the ridgetop moaned, while in the ruffled pool below the little frogs rested in silence. He looked up to see torn clouds racing north as if to join an oncoming battle.

"So, *Sikon Taleka*, already you know what is to come. A storm is gathering and by the signs, it will find this valley by day's end. Winter wants one more battle, little ones, and it may be you will see the sun rise through a glaze of ice."

Alonqua arose and made his way down to the pool's edge, where he knelt and splashed cool water on his face and arms.

"But my friends, this first Spring storm is Winter's last breath. He will retreat to his home of ice, far to the North. Before the Full Frog Moon rises you will sing again. This you know better than I.

"Mawenteh once told me we often speak the words we need to hear."

The boy stood and scanned the water's edge.

"I do not hear you, nor do I see you, but I feel your eyes. It is the same with my friend. Before I leave here I must tell you that while I slept a voice came to me. I think it was Mawenteh, but I did not hear the voice—only felt the word rise in my spirit, and the one word was 'prepare.'"

Alonqua stood and drew both hands to the medicine pouch which rested against his heart.

"Mawenteh, I heard you in my dreams. Now I ask that you hear me. I watched my father prepare for battle, sharpen his tomahawk, clean his gun, and paint his face red and black, the colors of war. It may be that I have heard your heart. I also prepare, not with war paint and weapon but as you would guide me, with sacred food and drink. Mawenteh, you said to me long ago that *Pamputis* was no enemy, and I know this storm is not my foe. I cannot hope to defeat her power. I cannot win, would not wish it if I could, but neither can I run away and hide. This storm knows me, and it will find me whether I run or rise to meet it."

Turning away from the pool, he walked up the rise to the last few embers of the little fire that had kept him warm through the long night. One last time he turned to the little forest pool and spoke.

"Sikon Taleka, we Lenape have no word for goodbye, so I will say, *lapich knewel...*until I see you! It may be I will not return here, but as long as I am alive, I will listen for you at winter's end."

Not until he turned to move up the ridge did Alonqua see her rising from a terrace of land just above him. He smiled as he strode to the ancient maple tree.

"*Ansikeme,* old friend, it is right that first I come to you! You remember I was here with Mawenteh on a warm spring afternoon after a cold night. Then your blood flowed fast like a little river. I am here once more and I have need of you. You whose roots lie deep in earth and stone, whose arms reach to the sky, I ask you the gift of your new life. Only a little. And in return I offer you the gift of gratitude."

Alonqua opened his medicine pouch and withdrew a smaller pouch of woven meadow grass. In each of the four directions his hands dug little openings in the earth, and into each he sprinkled tobacco. Bowing his head as he moved around the tree, he covered each offering and gave thanks. In the space between two great roots he found the box turtle shell and grooved stick

Mawenteh had placed there so long ago. Alonqua held the shell, bone white with age, until it grew warm in his hands, then set it down.

His knife lost, the flint fire-starter would have to serve. He first cut two converging channels, each a hand length long, through the bark and into the moist wood beneath. Where the two grooves met he used the point of the flint to bore out a narrow hole and into this wedged the stick. Alonqua held his breath and watched as little drops flowed down the grooves, met at the stick, and fell to the waiting shell. The boy touched the tree, bowed his head, and moved on to seek other gifts.

By the time Alonqua returned to *Ansikeme*, his buckskin top stuffed with spring harvest, the morning had passed. First, he drew out the little ground nuts of *otaes*, the soon-to-bloom spring flower, then the tightly curled tips of *ashikemensha,* fern. Last were the tender green shoots of *apawiak*, cattail. Each of these he had approached and gathered with reverence, departed in gratitude, leaving behind a pinch of tobacco.

By now the turtle shell cup was brimming over with sweet maple water, and before he reached down to taste, he plucked damp wads of fresh moss and pressed them into the wounds.

He took a deep drink from the shell and placed a hand on the tree.

"*Wanishi*, *Ansikeme*, for this gift of your new life."

When had eaten of the forest, meadow, and marsh, and finished with the last of the maple water, he lay back and saw that the racing clouds of morning had lowered and grown heavy, slowly swirling as if stirred by some vast hand. The air had grown still, the forest silent. Alonqua rose for the final task, for there was little time. The sassafras tree was not far, just up the slope, perched upon the ridgetop. Once there Alonqua looked out across the valley. The Great Marsh lay far below him, the waters mirroring the deepening gray of a troubled sky. Turning to the tree, Alonqua offered his hand to the deeply furrowed bark.

"I have not forgotten you, *Xaxakwe.* You are the Storm Tree, and I ask of you one last gift."

Alonqua open the little pouch and offered the last of his

tobacco to the silent tree.

"*Wanikwe*, Mawenteh thought no tree spirit more powerful. With the first spring thunder which shakes the Earth, you awaken; your roots come alive. And if the little frogs below offer the voice of the Creator, it is your root that offers the taste. The gift I ask of you is for my people. Safe in their shelters they will weather this storm. A much greater storm will follow. The old shelters will not stand in this storm of bullets and fire."

Alonqua knelt to see the place at the base of the tree where trunk and root joined. From there he moved his hand to the earth, and then outward from the tree as if tracing the course of a secret river. On hands and knees he followed the hidden root, until with a sharp stick he probed the earth. The flint blade scratched out a shallow trench the length of his arm—and there it was, a long thin tributary of the main root, the width of his thumb. He reached into the medicine pouch for his flint blade and placed it at his side.

"*Wanikwe,* my friend believed that when we gather from your roots just after the first spring thunder, and we drink of the tea made of the root, nothing good and true can be stolen from our hearts. Nothing deep within us will be forgotten—or ever truly die. From the West I hear the war drums grow stronger. The sky darkens! Do your roots feel the earth shake? Do your branches feel the sky tremble?"

As Alonqua knelt, blade in hand, the forest took in a breath and held it. Single shouts of thunder joined into the long, low growl of an angry bear, onrushing and relentless. The dark beast mounted the low ridge and surged down the valley side. The boy's fingers closed on the blade. A single drop of rain touched the root.

A blinding arrow of fire, a deafening roar shattered the air like a great stone hurled onto a sheet of ice.

Alonqua opened his eyes. He placed one trembling hand on the root, the other he reached toward the onrushing clouds.

"Now, *Xaxakwe*—now!"

Beneath the churning clouds, Alonqua cut from the root five pieces the length of his hand, then unwinding the red cord from his hair he gathered the roots and placed the bundle beneath his torn buckskin.

"*Wanishi, Xaxakwe,*" he whispered as he rose and approached the tree.

Lightning struck just below the ridge, followed the next instant with bone-shaking thunder. A sudden wind gust staggered the boy and he reached out to a low branch, while the other hand clutched the sacred roots near his heart.

"Stand with me, Mawenteh!"

The wind tore apart his words and flung them away.

"Mawenteh, I am afraid! The storm is too strong!"

Lightning raked the sky with fingers of white fire while a ripping crack of thunder, like one vast falling tree, split the air. The wind rose again, bore down on the boy, lashing him, tearing him from the tree and driving him to his knees. The clouds opened up and released the rain in drenching waves. Buffeted by thunder and wind, eyes glowing with the fire of the sky spears, Alonqua watched leafless trees bow and rise in homage to the storm, while far below the Great Marsh churned and frothed at the fury of its winds.

Alonqua turned his eyes to the roof of the storm, and he called out to the writhing clouds.

"*Pethakuwe!* Thunder-Beings! I hear your shouts! I see your war spears! I feel the breath of your wings of fire! Where are you? Show yourself!"

The storm swirled around him, revealing nothing but its power.

"Then I will find you!"

And so he offered his body to the storm, first walking, then running, allowing the wind to drive and carry him. As he breathed in the breath of the storm he closed his eyes, his body guided only by the wind and his heart. On and on he ran with the endless storm.

And then the storm paused as if to catch its breath. Breathless also, Alonqua sank to his knees. Down the ridge and through the pathless forest, he had come again to the Great Marsh, now to a thin point of land he had never seen. The wind returned with a hammering gust, as if the storm were a great hunting bear and had turned and found him there. Alonqua rose beneath her angry eyes and looked to the West where the faint golden light of a setting sun shone through a crease in the clouds and rain. The storm's fury swirled all about him, but the end was near.

Yet here and now, all around him the lightning struck hard, like blazing hammers. And the deafening war shouts of the Thunder-Beings rolled across marsh and through forest. Alonqua no longer ran; no power would move him. Heart pounding, hands clenched, he called out to the storm.

"*Pethakuwe!* Storm-fliers! Here! Look down! Alonqua is here!"

The answer was a strange cry, like the whinnying of a sky horse. Alonqua turned to the sound and called out once more.

"Is it you, *Pethakuwe*? Am I worthy now? What more must I do to see you?"

The cry again, nearer now, fearless, defiant, then wavering and distressed—the cries of a desperate mother.

Another spear of white fire ripped across the sky and Alonqua saw her—her shining head of snow and glistening body of the blackest night. In the heart of the sky-battle she drew in her wings, dove toward the water, leveled off, and thrust them deep into the blocking wind. One slow heavy stroke, then another, another, coming faster now, another, another...but just as she reached the boy on the shore the great bird pulled up, talons clenched, eyes on fire, Alonqua called out to her.

"*Opalanie!*"

Alonqua felt the breath of her wings on his face as she rose just above him. This was not the Thunder-Being—not the *Pethakuwe*. She was *Opalanie*, the Eagle, and she had found him.

Opalanie soared out over the marsh and then again back toward the shore. Finding a crease in the raging wind, she rose to the crown of a great oak. Just as she thrust out her talons to join a dark mass of sticks, she looked to the clouds, cried out and veered away from the nest.

Far below the living air buzzed and sizzled; Alonqua's unbound hair floated from his shoulders. His hands clenched the bundled roots just as the arrow of fire struck the tall tree, shattering the crown into crackling golden sparks.

This boy, both touched and blinded by the strike, likely did not see the tree explode, the nest destroyed. And if he did, he would never speak of it, nor the fiery wings of the *Pethakuwe* he had so longed to see. Too dazed to feel the pain, he would not recall how he struggled to his feet, managed a few stumbling steps, and collapsed, one hand still clutching the bundled roots, the other a charred stick. It is certain he did not see the wisp of smoke rise from his shoulder, for now his mind was lost on a dark river.

From this river he could not know of the sky battle still raging for a time, then moving on, did not see the pulses of light, nor hear the fading war shouts of the Thunder-Beings as they soared on to the East. The boy did not feel the rain cease, the winds grow still, the clouds part. He could not watch the moonlight transform the rain-touched forest into a sea of silver stars. Nor did the boy feel the gentle touch of the moon upon his wounded shoulder.

It is good he had not yet seen the charred crown of the great oak—still glowing, still smoking—nor the scattered sticks below, nor the one held in his hand. But the moonlight, as it always does, fell gently upon all that lay beneath her—upon the boy, upon the tree, the shattered nest, and upon the mother as she flew silently through the night, unable to rest, grieving her storm-broken nest, mourning her empty spring.

CHAPTER 10
SPIRIT NAME

Only the calls of the awakening birds signaled the return of the light. Far up, hidden in the crown of a swamp elm, a little bird launched herself, shaking loose a drop of rain from her perch. The drop slid down a twig, fell to a branch awakening other drops that joined in a flowing thread, a silver-gray rivulet that flowed down, spilling off one branch and onto another until it was free to reach the earth and the cheek of a sleeping boy.

Alonqua touched his face and opened his eyes to the still marsh, hidden in a sea of cold mist.

He lifted his other hand and saw the blackened stick. When he braced himself to sit up, a searing pain in his shoulder drove him to lie back and be still. He lifted his free hand to feel beneath the buckskin, then withdrew it, not prepared for what he might find.

Again, he struggled to rise, and fell back from the hurt. Breathing hard, biting his lip, he rested his head upon a tuft of grass and waited for the fiery pain to ease. He raised the stick and held it to his eyes, then turned his head to see a great oak tree rising out of the mist, the smoldering top broken like a blackened tooth. He closed his eyes. His voice was silent, lost in his breath-mist, but his mouth formed the words.

"*Gitchi Manito*—why do you allow this?"

There was no answer, not in the trees, nor in the air, nor in the silent brooding marsh.

Slowly, as if his body might break, Alonqua rose to one arm and pushed himself upright. Squinting through pain, his eyes searched the ground beneath the stricken tree. In all directions lay the sticks, many charred black. With the stick he held as support, he willed his legs to stand and looked up to the empty place where there had once been a nest. Pointing the stick to the gray sky he spoke hard words, like the stone-words of his father the morning he left to fight, bitter and alone.

"*Gitchi Manito!* I found my way through the Place of the Frozen Heart. I found the Healing Tree. Her wound healed and the healing place held life."

He shook the stick at the shattered tree.

"*Manito!* This tree will not heal! This tree is dead. This tree, so ancient and wise, will not see this spring nor any other!"

He was not done; his voice grew soft, but no less cold.

"This tree held its own life. And it held the life of another—and of her mate—and of little ones not yet born. You release *Pethakuwe* and their white spears of fire—and all are gone. This great Tree! The nest! The eggs! The mother, too? I do not point this stick of shame at *Pamputis.* I do not shake it at Pethakuwe. The Thunder-Beings do what you bid them to do. Even the Whites whose sickness killed my mother, whose bullets killed my father, hold less blame than You. You have power to stop them. Now I know my father's heart when he went to war. He knew well we could not win this battle. He knew he would die."

The boy raked the charred stick hard across both cheeks until red blood joined the black streaks. Again he lifted the stick to the clouds.

"*Manito!* It is You who allow this! It is You who..."

Alonqua's words died in his throat when he saw her. The accusing stick fell from his hand. She had appeared from nowhere, silently, as true gifts do. At first she was but a shadow, tall and still, resting on a dark branch above the scattered ruins. A white crown rose above the shadow, and the eyes which turned toward his—first one and then the other—glowed yellow like the sun.

"Opalanie," he whispered.

A distant cry—another eagle—turned her attention from the boy to the sky, where even now her mate was calling. She did not answer.

If there was a desire to share his wounds with her, Alonqua remained silent; she had no need of his pain, nor he of hers. To be with her now was enough. Another call and she stretched out her neck and responded, the quavering tone subdued, mournful.

But she did not leave to join her husband. There would be time for that, and he did not call again. She again turned her eyes on the boy, and the two remained there together, each regarding the other until the sun cleared the ridge, and a misty, soft, golden light sifted its way through the forest. *Opalanie* turned her eyes to the East, spread her great wings wide and shook off the morning dew in a spray of glistening mist. Alonqua watched as she descended from her perch to the remains of the nest. Amid the sticks lay scattered flecks of white. One of these she lifted gently in her beak, dropped it, and went to another, then another. Only when those too small to lift remained untouched did she direct her eyes once more to the boy, first to his eyes, then to the ground beneath his feet.

Alonqua looked down and saw the charred stick, still resting where he had dropped it, and he knew. He bent low, lifted the stick, and held it out to her, as one would offer a precious gift. She remained still until he placed the gift on the sacred earth and backed away.

The stick was large, larger than the rest. It was the first piece, the foundation around which the nest grew. One step, then another, and another, and yet one more and she was there. The wind ruffled the white feathers of her crown, then lifted the black hair of the boy from his brow. Her talon, yellow like her eyes and tipped with curved jet-black claws, clutched the stick. And only then did she look to the sky and call to her mate.

Her prize well-secured, she opened her great wings, and with powerful strokes rose above the blasted tree, circled it once, and soared away to join her partner. Alonqua ran to the water's edge to follow her path. Halfway across the marsh the eagles met and together flew swiftly to the East, toward the Sacred Springs, toward *Ahsen* and his Bride. The one who carried the charred stick led the way. And her head shone like the morning star.

Alonqua shielded his eyes as she melted away in the glare of the newly risen sun.

Turning his eyes away, Alonqua looked to the North where already a wall of iron-gray clouds was rising. Fingers of cold touched his skin. For a time the earth would feel winter's final breath. A gathering of swallows danced above the water, seeking newly-risen spring midges. Alonqua took in a long breath, released it slowly. When he spoke to them the words were soft.

"Soon you will be chasing snowflakes, my friends, but the cold will only be a moment. It will not last. You will live and raise your young in warm winds. *Sikon Taleka* is silent now, but she will soon sing once more."

He turned back to the shattered tree, wisps of smoke still rising from the crown. Around him lay the scattered fragments of the broken nest.

"This, too, is not the end. The story will go on. A seed from this tree will sprout. A new tree will rise in a pool of new sunlight."

Kneeling, he reached out to hold a piece of white shell.

"And there will be another nest. The mother carries now the seed to plant upon another tree. And the nest will grow. And she has found her mate, and she will carry within her the seeds of new life."

Placing the shell gently upon a stone, Alonqua rose and faced the sun.

"*Gitchi Manito,* I ask you to forgive my anger—*Wanishi, Opalanie,* — you have shown the way to live with courage."

As he rose he looked back to the place where the eagle had risen. From where he stood what he saw appeared as another broken shell, only larger, whiter, glowing even under the dark sky. As he drew close Alonqua's eyes widened. Where there was once a charred stick rested a delicate broad leaf of purest white, nearly the size of a child's hand.

Slowly, slowly, Alonqua reached out and slid both hands beneath the feather, and drew the gift close to his eyes. The filaments danced under his breath as if alive, and so fearing this offering might rise and fly away, he placed one hand gently upon the other. The hand that cradled the feather trembled, and Alonqua's eyes searched the forest, as if aware of some unseen presence.

"Mawenteh, you are near. From the moment your spirit was free I have looked for you. And now I feel your heart hold mine, as these hands hold the gift of *Opalanie*."

He opened his hands slightly and held them to the sky.

"Do you see? A gift from Mother Eagle...Can you see my own mother, Mawenteh? Does she smile?"

The wind was shifting, pouring down now from the North, down the valley like the rush of a vast sky river. Alonqua shielded the feather and held it close to his heart.

"Mawenteh, before I left your side—I cannot forget—you spoke to me that my journey would hold two wonders. The first would release your spirit. You spoke that the second wonder would reveal mine…Is this…?"

Still holding *Opalanie's* gift close, he spoke with trembling voice.

"Mawenteh! No! I have not the strength to hold the spirit that rests in my hand. I have not the eyes and heart of the Eagle—my journey has only now begun. I have to learn to be wise—I have not yet earned this name! I am only a boy!"

The feather was now a red coal in his hands, and he opened them to release the pain. And now the ember was again a feather, cool and white, free to go another more worthy. A strong gust pushed hard at his back, but his body formed a little eddy in the river of wind, and the feather floated and danced within reach of a boy's hand. And there it stayed—until a man's hand reached out to bring it home.

As Alonqua placed the feather gently within the soft folds of his medicine pouch, careful to give the gift room to unfurl and breathe, he smiled a smile of peace. And he spoke in a voice now firm and steady.

"I remember a time, Mawenteh, when your body was still strong enough to do the work of your youth. You spoke to me at the end of a long autumn day. Together we had worked hard, and together we put in place the last strip of elm bark for our winter dwelling. You took me aside, praised my work, said to me that many men had not the skill I had shown."

Alonqua, still smiling, shook his head.

"I remember feeling I had done only what anyone would do in my place, so I answered your praise with a shrug—and that did not please you. Not at all! You came to me and squared my shoulders. You waited until you held my eyes and then you spoke. You said that it is not your way to offer worthless praise, and that praise from the heart is a gift not to be cast away with the shrug of a shoulder. I was about to tell you I was sorry, but you silenced me.

"Your next words—I hear them now: 'Alonqua, you are young. But even now you know no man truly rises above another. You have humility, and I honor that in you. But even a humble man must know his own worth. There are times he must accept praise with grace and respect the gifts the Great Spirit has placed within his heart. And then he must live in a way to use these gifts for the good of all. My son, I ask you not to demean your spirit with your doubt.'"

The cold wind clawed at him as he placed the pouch beneath his buckskin top. His smile faded, but his eyes remained full of light.

"Mawenteh, just before the storm, when I thought I had need of you, I called for help. You did not come but as a voice that was soon lost in the winds. Now the storm has passed, and you answer when I do not ask. That is how it must be for us. I will look after my own spirit—you after yours. When you come, it will be as now—out of need, not want—not to shelter me, but to point the way I have known all along."

The feather safely tucked away, Alonqua moved his hand to his shoulder, then under the singed buckskin to the wound. Eyes shut and teeth clenched, he awaited the searing pain that never came. There was no raw flesh, nothing but the ridge of a scar. Alonqua withdrew his hand and looked out across the marsh, where even now the eagles were hard at work. The new nest must rise quickly for the young to fledge before autumn. But they had found the tree, and the first stick was strong, hardened by fire.

There was nothing holding him here but still he lingered.

"Yes," he whispered to his heart. "That will be a good thing."

Alonqua found the shell fragment he had left on the stone. As he knelt to gather soft grass to keep it safe, he uncovered an acorn born of the stricken tree. Smiling, he placed the acorn upon the shell and formed a nest around both, and gently nestled this gift deep within his pouch.

Alonqua turned his eyes away from the marsh, toward the South, to his village. He held out his hands to those who awaited his return.

"I am called Alonqua."

His eyes returned to the marsh, and then up to a place beyond the clouds where one might see an eagle, head and tail shining under the sun.

"I am called Sapelei Opalanie... "

Then there came with the rising wind the deep rhythm of forgotten drums—at one with the heart of Shining Eagle.

Part Two

CHAPTER 11

AHSENA PAHSAK

Had Alonqua chosen to return to the village, by nightfall he would be home. Awaiting him were his people, still mourning his friend, but eager to hear of his journey. Though cold rain stung his face and arms, and his legs longed for rest, he kept moving. To stop now would mean unending sleep.

Along deer paths through the forest Alonqua plucked basswood and hawthorn buds from low branches and chewed them slowly. Some early mushrooms poked their caps above the sodden leaves. They were the good ones; Mawenteh had taught him well. Despite a waist-deep river crossing, by the time he reached the river path to the village, some of his strength had returned. In the gray misty forest he paused and looked toward the village. At his feet a creek flowed across the path. Large stones had been placed in the creek bed for easy crossing, but he turned away from them and the village beyond.

Instead the little stream became his path. Over untold winters the fast-flowing water had carved a deep ravine not far from the village. Just beyond its narrowest point the gorge widened into what Alonqua's people called *Ahsena Pahsak*, the Valley of Stones, a sacred ground perched high above the marsh and river. If, as many believed, the *Kuwi Awen*, spirits of the ancient ones, remained there, perhaps they turned ghostly eyes to see a lone figure enter their domain as the last light of day passed from the ridgetop.

But just as Alonqua entered the dark valley he froze and dropped to his knees, not for fear of the dead, but at the smell of smoke. On hands and knees, he crept silent as a shadow from bush to stone until he could see a clear distance. An arrow's flight away, jutting out from the valley-side was a great stone the size of a lodge house. Beneath the rock lay a shadowed recess. and at its center rose a low steady flame.

Alonqua smiled as he rose from his crouch.

"Mawenteh, are you near?" whispered Alonqua. "I recall what you taught me. This is not a White Man's fire. It is much too small."

Halving the distance to the fire, Alonqua stopped and called out, "*Heh*!"

A stirring from the dark place—a faint silhouette rose before the flames.

"*Heh! Nee* Alonqua! Who greets me with a warm fire?"

"Alonqua! Alonqua! *Nee* Temetet! You are here. River-bird Woman spoke the truth."

"Temetet, my friend!"

The boy left the fire and clambered down from the shelter; he met Alonqua already halfway up the slope. They clasped hands and searched each other's eyes.

"*Kayah*, Alonqua…"

"*Maheelah,* Temetet! I agree. It is a wonder we meet here."

Seeing his friend clad only in torn buckskin and leggings, Temetet motioned to the shelter.

"Alonqua, come to the fire. There is food."

Temetet reached across to support his friend as they made their way up the steep slope, then eased Alonqua down upon a smooth stone bench by the fire. After placing new wood on the embers he set a clay bowl of cornmeal and venison alongside the flames. Alonqua watched the steam curl above the bowl as from behind he felt a fur cape draped across his shoulders, then suddenly pulled away.

"Alonqua, your buckskin! The shoulder is black and torn, touched by flames. Are you hurt? Let me look beneath."

Retrieving the cape and covering both shoulders he offered

his friend a sheepish smile.

"I got a little too close to a fire—nothing more. Not a wise thing to do. But it is healing well."

"Too close to a fire? Alonqua, let me look—there must be a…"

Gripping the cape tightly around his neck, Alonqua held out his hand.

"No, Temetet—no need—believe me. I was burned. The wound has healed. No need to look…"

One look into Alonqua's eyes and Temetet knew the matter was closed. He sat opposite Alonqua, across the fire, his eyes fixed on his friend, regarding him as he watched his pale hands reach for the steaming bowl of food, bow his head and begin to eat. Temetet saw his friend's eyes turn inward and close while he lifted morsel after morsel to his mouth, chewing slowly, gratefully. When at last Alonqua placed the empty bowl at his side, Temetet leaned toward his friend, as if to speak once more. Again he sat back and looked away.

"What is it, my friend? Speak what is in your heart."

"You are changed, Alonqua." He rose to hand Alonqua a water pouch and returned to his place across the fire.

"Hiding a wound—that I understand. I also do not want others to view my hurts when I know I can tend them myself. This is what we are taught. But your eyes, your voice are not the same as I knew them. I fear my friend is gone, and another sits here."

Alonqua raised the pouch, drank deep and tossed it back to Temetet.

"The water I drink—the stream below from which it came—this fire—its warmth. This food—you, Temetet, my friend—sitting right there across the fire which warmed the food. The stone above and beneath—lit by the fire. Somewhere near—in the darkness—there rests a village—our village. These things are what I know—nothing more. You speak of my eyes—of a change. I cannot see what you see, but I believe you. If I had the words I would tell you what they have seen. It would ease my heart."

A few spring snowflakes drifted in from the darkness and vanished above the flames.

"But tell me, Temetet—say to me you could you speak of a dream before you wake."

Temetet shook his head and looked away, knowing well, as all his people know, what must be left unsaid—what is sacred to one who has returned from a vision-quest.

"But now I ask you, Temetet, why you are here—as if you were waiting for me?"

"It was River-bird Woman," offered Temetet, as if eager to change paths, "who said you would come to this place. She said you would have need of a friend, and asked that I tend the fire and wait."

Alonqua smiled. "I should have known that a piece of Mawenteh's heart lives in the heart of his wife—and that his spirit directed me here. Temetet, where does Mawenteh's body rest?"

Temetet pulled a burning stick from the fire, stood at the lip of the shelter, and directed the torchlight down to several flat stones resting on an earthen terrace.

"Mawenteh's body lies beneath the stones."

"So he chose this place—in the Valley of Stones. He never spoke of this to me."

"No one knew his wish—not even his wife—until his last words were spoken."

Alonqua searched the woodpile for the driest stick and held one end in the flames. Picking his way down the ledge he approached the burial stones and knelt. Again a gathering of snowflakes hovered and spun in the torchlight like little moths. Alonqua placed his hand upon each stone, seven in all. As the torch light flickered and faded, his eyes grew hard like the stones beneath his hand.

"Where are the gifts?" Alonqua spat out his bitter words as he climbed back to the shelter and stood by the fire "This man loved his people. He was loved. No one knows this better than I. There should be gifts upon the stone—a gift from each man, each woman, each child of the village! Where are the bowls of food for his journey? There is nothing—Temetet, say there were words spoken honoring Mawenteh! Say that the women performed the sacred dance while they raised their eyes and chanted to the stars."

Temetet rose and stood before his friend. He offered his hand but it was brushed away.

"Alonqua, I thought you knew! I would have told you sooner."

"What? Told me what!? He is Mawenteh! The heart-gatherer. Who deserves this more?"

"No one! Alonqua, we were waiting for you…just as Mawenteh wished. After you left his side I was told Mawenteh lay silent until the rain stopped and the sky cleared...that near the end he opened his eyes and asked to be carried out so that he might see the stars. As they bore his body to a place of darkness, they placed soft furs on the wet earth, and lay him down upon them. He asked them to leave him, all save his wife. But before they left him he asked that his body be taken here, in the Valley of Stones, at the rising of the sun. He asked that his body be buried in the soft earth terrace below the great shelter, but that the ceremony await your return. One thing more—I remember River-bird Woman spoke to me about Mawenteh's eyes. That as his spirit passed his head turned to the West, his eyes still on the stars. She said to me that his eyes were searching for you."

At the peak of the sky the moon found a crease in the clouds. Beneath the silver light two hands met, clasped, and held on. Alonqua's hard words melted to a soft whisper.

"Forgive me, Temetet." His free hand reached toward the sleeping village near the river. "My people—forgive—Mawenteh would not be pleased. He would say to me that a child speaks before understanding, but a man waits to speak until he knows. In the morning I accuse *Manito*—and at night, my own people. Both without cause. So I have changed? Look again, my friend, at this child who stands before you."

"No child speaks these words, Alonqua. I am young, but I can see and hear. Now my work is to go to the village you left and tell the people of your return. The people will rejoice at my news, and they will begin to prepare the ceremony at dawn. At day's end we will come here."

Just as Temetet placed cold hands above the warming fire, he turned once again to Alonqua with the toothy excited smile he knew so well. "But wait! I have a thought, Alonqua! Return with me! We two will receive a welcome like no other. We will be *kanshoweneh*—great men—you who have returned from a great journey; I who was here to save you!"

"What an idea, Temetet! And while we walk the river path, the stories can grow very large."

"Yes! Do you recall how you fought a two-headed frog in the marsh? The size of a bear!"

"Yes! Or that you found me, near death, beneath the branches of a great fallen tree—and you called upon great powers, lifted the tree, threw it aside like a toy, and carried me to safety!"

"And Alonqua! You can say how you were carried by the storm to a far-off land, and that you returned on the wings of an eagle!" Their echoing laughter faded into the darkness. Alonqua turned away. His words came from a distant place.

"That storm you speak of—that storm was real. You were here, sheltered in this valley beneath this stone roof. Even so you must have felt its power. Temetet—that storm swallowed me."

Alonqua turned his eyes to the dying fire.

"You go on to the village. Tell them I am well, but that I must be here."

"Alonqua, I was only joking, as you know I love to do. I never meant..."

"You have done nothing wrong, my friend—nor I when I joined you in your game. Just now we were two little boys chasing away the dark, and it felt good—even for a moment. But now that is past. And your words of the storm brought back to me what I know. I cannot go to the village—I am very tired. And you cannot stay—they must know this night I have come home."

They looked out past the little dome of firelight where beneath the moonlight, snow-dusted stones rose like ghosts from the shadows.

"Alonqua, I am eager to see the village, but I do not wish to leave you here alone. I have been here alone two nights. This night—drums!—like faraway thunder—just before I saw you. The spirits roam these stones. I feel their eyes,"

"Temetet, I have felt these eyes before I entered the valley. I think I have felt them the moment my journey began. I feel them now. Upon every stone the spirits stand and wait. They mean us no harm. Travel in peace, Temetet. Trust the night that all will be well."

The night drew close. The moon floated just above the eastern ridge. Somewhere in the deep forest, *Ghokos,* the Owl cried out his quavering lonely message to the night.

"*Lapich Knewell*, my friend—until I see you. Tell the people I rejoice at their coming. But I ask they delay until the sun is low. I need this night to rest—the next to gather my heart. I trust they will understand."

"They will. We will need to prepare no less than you. *Lapich knewell*, Alonqua. There is food here, and warm furs."

Two hands clasped in the glow of the fading fire. Temetet turned and clambered down the gravel slope. Just before he was swallowed by the stone-shadows, Alonqua cried out to his friend,

"*He*, Temetet! Bring back a new buckskin—and leggings!"

The responding laugh was lost in the darkness. And Alonqua's smile faded as he fed the embers with fresh wood. Once again, the flames rose to tell the story of the trees, of green leaves open to the sun, of wind and storms, of cold and ice—of birds and squirrels that played among the swaying branches. Alonqua heard the story and smiled as he looked out past the firelight and into the darkness beyond.

"So, spirits of the stones, you are here. Mawenteh spoke to me of you—only once—here, only last Spring. Do you remember? I sat then where I sit now. Mawenteh, stood—there—between the fire and the dark. He spoke of you as The Old Ones, and that yours are the spirits of a people who lived and died here long, long ago. A time of summer ice. A time of ceaseless wind and storm. He spoke of you as great hunters contesting with mighty beasts."

The sky had cleared. Alonqua stood and moved away from the flames and looked up at the stars, suspended like silver jewels across the blue-black sky.

"He said you were here so long ago, that these same stars have wandered, that I would not know the night sky you then looked upon. You must remember that I asked him why you, The Old Ones, still linger here in the Valley of Stones, why your spirits are not with those who build their campfires along the River of Stars. He said he did not know—for certain—but what felt in his heart to be true arrived to him as visions, waking dreams—Mawenteh felt in his heart that we who have traveled from the East, we carry your blood in our veins, and that you have waited here for us to return to our true home."

A night wind flowed down the valley. In the little openings between stones dry leaves funneled and hissed.

"He knew nothing more than what he spoke, and of what he spoke he could not be sure. That is the reason he had shared this with no one, not even his wife. Mawenteh believed this was not a time to share dream-visions when our hearts must be centered just to survive. But he wanted me to know, and I asked him why. He smiled and shook his head. 'My work is nearly done. Yours has begun.' Mawenteh pointed to the fire. 'Can a new fire rise from this old one? You know the answer. A new fire will rise, and you will tend it.' Mawenteh looked at me—through my eyes into my heart. I knew his meaning without knowing. It was trust. And because I trusted, I never spoke of that night again—until now. Nor did Mawenteh speak about it—until his last words for me on this Earth. Just as I left his side, he called me back. He took my hand, held it with the grip of a strong man, drew me close, 'It is time to relight the fire.'"

Alonqua looked down to the burial place hidden in darkness.

"Mawenteh, are you near? Am I speaking to the Old Ones? To you? Both? Do you take your place among the Old Ones? Or have you already journeyed to the stars where you rest?

Again *Ghokos* called, closer now, as if he, too, sought warmth on that cold spring night. Alonqua turned back to the fire, fed the flames one last time, banked it, and sat down. His yawn was profound. Between the bench and the fire was room to stretch. Alonqua spread a soft fur the stone and lay down, pulling a thinner fur over him. He lay still for a time, placing both hands on his heart, as he often did.

Very soon his hands, first one, then the other, slipped to his sides and he slept.

Much later the moon dipped low. Her light glimmered for a time through the treetops, faded, and was gone.

And then from a place beyond the owl, beyond the forest, beyond the marsh, perhaps beyond any place on Earth, rose the cry from the night—long, quavering call, starting low, ending high, very old and alone. Alonqua shivered and his eyes flickered open. He rose and peered into the darkness. Silence. Pulling the furs tight around his shoulders he lay back down, drew in a slow breath, and once again placed both hands on his heart.

Someone sitting beside him, someone awake, might then have heard the slow beat of distant drums rising and falling somewhere deep in this moonless night. But Alonqua did not hear, could not hear. His mind was far away, drifting on the peaceful river of sleep. But…

his heart…

his heart…

his heart…

slow now…

steady…

twined her beat around the pulse of the ancient drums, as Alonqua slept near the fire in the heart of *Ahsen Pahsak*—the Valley of Stones.

CHAPTER 12

BETWEEN WORLDS

Alonqua stretched beneath the warm fur and opened his eyes. There was little to see, a stone ceiling above him, to one side a dark stone wall, to the other a soft gray wall of mist. He drew in a long breath and let it out. The air was chill and damp, as if it were the breath of the old stones. All lay still—the lone sound the distant voice of flowing water.

Dawn had come late here, as it always had. Even as morning light was spreading across the land, here, in the Valley of Stones, shrouded by the fog, the sun appeared driven-off, locked away.

"Where there is no sun, there should be fire," whispered Alonqua.

He rose from the soft furs and blew on the ashes of the old fire, exposing the cluster of embers that lay in its heart. A few twigs, a few breaths—and so two fires, one of wood, one of spirit, rose from the ashes of a long night.

As Alonqua watched the flames grow, felt the warmth upon his hand and face, his soft words broke the silence of the morning.

"Grandfather Fire, gift of *Kishelamukong,* you awaken—as you have so many times. The Old Ones who are here draw near you, feel the warmth once again you have received from the sun.

"*Wanishi* for your living presence here, you who have risen from the gray cold ashes of the old life to dancing flames and new beginnings."

As Alonqua carefully placed more sticks on the eager fire,

the flames and the morning mist rose together. Nearby stones appeared, then more distant trees, and then, his eyes on the brightening sky to the East, Alonqua removed his tattered buckskin top and breechcloth. Slowly, reverently, he lowered these, and his worn moccasins, to the flames. His medicine pouch he placed on the stone bench, alongside the bundle of twigs bound with the blood-red cord. He remained near the fire, turning his body this way and that, clothing his body with the smoke of the past. He added more wood and addressed the flames.

"*Wanishi*, Grandfather Fire. What I held from my past you no longer need to burn away. My days as a child are gone, yet what I have learned as a child lives on. Now it is time I seek your Sister."

As Alonqua picked his way among the stones, he did not see the dark smoke from smoldering buckskin rise high above the flames. He reached the little stream where the water gathered in a swirling pool and his voice joined the music of the flow.

"Spirit of the water—you are the lifeblood of the Earth and to all that lives upon it. You are soft but you carve mountains. It is you we call upon to bring sleep to Grandfather Fire. It is you we call upon to cleanse our body and spirit—to refresh our hearts and begin our life with each sunrise. *Wanishi*!"

Alonqua entered the water with eyes closed. As he reached the heart of the pool he knelt, and from cupped hands lifted the chill water and released it, first upon his heart, then upon his head, and last upon the scar across his shoulder. Trembling like a sapling in the winter wind, he stretched out on his back and invited the water to cradle his body and enter his heart.

Just as the sun rose above the ridge Alonqua rose from the water. The few shoals of mist tangled amid stones and trees were touched with gold. When he returned to the fire a moment later, his buckskin top and breechcloth were consumed, save for their black shadow upon the gray ashes. Stirring the ashes with a stick, Alonqua knelt before the bed of embers.

"Mawenteh, your name means 'heart-gatherer.' And that is what you did. You gathered my heart when I was a child and alone. You have gathered the hearts of the village—not as chief, but as a kind man. You are gone, where I do not know. Sometimes I feel you close. Mostly I feel alone. I cannot ask you now to gather again my lonely heart. This is something I must do."

Rising from the fire Alonqua lifted the fur from the stone and wrapped himself in its warmth. He reached for the medicine pouch and released the cords.

First to emerge from the folds was a snowy-white feather, soft as air. This Alonqua placed at his side.

Then, humming his mother's lullaby, he reached in the pouch and found the black shard from the Cradle of Wood, forged by lightning, hard as flint. And as he sang of the Island of Light and the Tree of Life, he moved his hand beneath the fur, closed his eyes and held the gift lightly upon his scarred shoulder.

"May the wounds of my people, the ones past, the ones now, and the hurts to come, heal. And in the place of healing may new life find a home."

Alonqua opened his eyes and placed the gift of the healing tree on a warm, flat stone near the fire.

Returning his hand to the medicine pouch, he searched until he found the smooth, oval ear-stone of *kwenkankale.* He held the gift in his palm, drew it up close, and at once, his eyes lit up with wonder.

"Brother fish! Or better—Uncle! Mawenteh said your ear-stone holds the story of your life—where you were born, where you traveled, your good days and not-so-good ones. He showed me how your ear-stones can be read to reveal how long you have lived—that each winter leaves a ring, a little darker than the pure-white. *Kwenkankale*! You have seen many winters! Let me see—*telen...nininxke...zintxke*...more than thirty summers you swam the waters! What adventures! And now you swim in the River of Stars! May you find adventure there as well—each time I touch this stone as I do now, you will hear me speak of your coming home at the passing of your spirit—*maxelintamewaken*! I honor you!"

The white ear-stone took its place beside the black tree-scar, and once again, Alonqua searched the pouch, this time finding the gift of the mother otter. As he held the inner shell to the morning sun, gossamer rainbows shimmered like a sunrise.

"*Ehes*! When *Kwenoomuk* left me your shell I thought only of her, not of you! And now I think of the wonder in living in a house so smooth and beautiful. Could you see what I see? The colors of your walls? How could you know without eyes? Without light? Somehow you knew. This came from you. You painted these colors—they come from you, are a part of you. Your body was a gift to *Kwenoomuk,* and your spirit leaves her beauty here, under the sun you had never seen. My friend spoke often of the Great Mystery—Mawenteh, is not this shell at its heart?"

Alonqua placed the gift alongside the ear-stone. His eyes turned toward the river, toward the marsh beyond.

"*Kwenoomuk*, I think I hear you and your children playing in some deep pool hidden by reeds. May your pain, your little ones' fear, fade day by day. Soon your children will leave your side, seeking their own fish and their own lives. Soon you will have more pups—and if not now, next spring—*Wanishi* for your trust in me. I felt the touch and sound of my own mother's arms, but I was too young to know how deeply she loved me. *Kwenoomuk,* I treasure your lesson. Now I know."

The next gift of the medicine pouch was still damp, and so he placed the sweetgrass near the fire to dry out. Again, Alonqua looked out toward the marsh where the morning sun graced a home of sticks and mud.

"Someday, *Temakwe,* when I build my own *wikiwam* with my hands—when the walls and roof are sealed from wind and rain—when I receive the first visitor who seeks shelter—one who is cold and tired. When that happens I will find my medicine pouch, and I will reach in for this sweetgrass, and I will catch the end on fire—and I will invite my guest to breathe in the sweet smoke of kindness. May I always live to do as you do—offer a place to one in need—and to protect what is sacred."

Last to emerge from the pouch was the little nest of soft marsh grass which held a shell fragment cradling an acorn. Alonqua held it a long time, but found no words, as though they lived in a story not yet told.

Alonqua turned his eyes from a place too distant to see except in his heart—to the white feather resting at his side. But though this was close, he held the feather closer, as if to find somewhere enmeshed in its shaft and filaments the answer to an unknown question.

"*Opalanie,* what does your gift say to me? At this moment only this—if otter shows me a mother's love, you show me the courage to love when all is lost—the courage to choose the strongest of what remains, leave behind the rest—and begin again."

Having spoken these words, Alonqua untied the red cord from the bundle of roots. He took one end of the cord and made a little loop and held it against the lower shaft of the feather. Rotating the shaft, he coiled the cord down the shaft to the tip, pushed the loose end through the loop and pulled tight. He tossed back his night-black hair and bound it tight with the remaining cord.

"Black, red, white," whispered Alonqua. "Strength, faith, and light. This is a good beginning."

One by one, first the gift of the Healing Tree, then the ear-stone of the old fish, the iridescent shell of *Ehes,* the tuft of sweetgrass, the eggshell and acorn, fruits of his quest, entered the pouch, and his heart. And he pulled tight the drawstrings of both.

Alonqua placed the pouch along with the sassafras roots in recess in the wall. The morning was growing old, and the spring sun was high and strong. The traces of night snow had vanished, and wisps of steam rose from the old stones. Alonqua placed a few sticks on the fire, more for the companionship of the flames than warmth.

As he turned his eyes toward the village beyond the ridge, he smiled and shook his head.

"My people—on the river trail. You carry food in clay pots, gifts held close to your hearts. I know you bring drums for the dancing! Haha! Temetet! May you arrive first! With leggings and vest. To join the dance as I am would take more courage than I will ever have!"

As the sun climbed to its highest place, Alonqua reached beneath the fur and placed his hand on his heart. The beat was steady and strong; his heart gathered in a single drum. Soon he would hear the sounds of his people ascending the little stream, their voices soft as drifting clouds. He knew they would not be long in coming. But for now he closed his eyes.

CHAPTER 13
THE GLOWING RING

Each time the shadow crossed his face his eyelids twitched ever so slightly. And then came the cry, shrill and quavering, a whinny like a wounded sky-horse. Only then did he open his eyes and see the eagle skim the treetops and soar across the sun.

"*Opalanie!*" breathed Alonqua.

He stood, the warm furs falling to the cold stone. His eyes tracked the lone eagle as she wheeled back and forth above the Valley of Stones. Each time she approached the sun his one hand shielded his eyes, while the other moved to touch the snow-white feather at rest on his shoulder.

"My dream before waking was of you, *Opalanie*, flying beneath the golden sun. Why you come to me I would wish to know, but what matters is that you are here."

Once more she passed over him. Once more she called out, and then, just as he raised his hand to honor her, she was gone.

"*Opalanie,* I wished to ask whether your blackened stick rests in a strong tree deep within a new nest. But I know you hear me. The season is late to begin again, but I will pray to *Manito* that young eagles will be testing their wings by summer's end."

A hand touched his shoulder. Alonqua spun around to see Temetet's toothy grin and laughing eyes.

"Temetet! The least you could do is to show yourself to my face instead of…"

"What, come openly while you were looking up and

whispering to the air? You surely have changed, Alonqua. There was a time you would have sensed my coming without eyes. Now you seem not in the world I walk in—haha, I shiver in the wind! And I have buckskin and leggings! And you?"

Alonqua looked down to see the blanket at his feet.

"I am here, as you can well—too well—see, Temetet, and I do very much feel the cold wind, and I do not wish to greet the village like this and if you would stop laughing and hand me what you brought I would be grateful!"

Still smiling, Temetet placed in his friend's hands a bundle bound with sinew, then stood away.

"You had best dress quickly then, or you will have what you do not wish. The People are close behind. I will build up the fire, while you prepare yourself."

The bundle unbound, Alonqua laid out the fine elk skin leggings, buckskin top, moccasins, and a breechcloth of brushed doeskin adorned with delicate beadwork. Alonqua's eyes widened as he encircled his waist with a narrow belt of soft hide.

"Who made this design? Was it River-bird Woman?"

"Alonqua, what are you whispering about? Hurry and dress! I think I hear the people!"

Alonqua's eyes lingered upon the breechcloth, moving from the beaded eagle to the jagged streak of yellow lightning, then back to the fierce yellow eye of *Opalanie.*

"How could she know?"

"Alonqua, again whispering to no one! Hurry! I hear them!"

Breathless Alonqua tucked the narrow center of the piece between his thighs and drew the front and back flap over the leather belt tied around his waist. First one legging than the other followed, attaching the tops of both with thongs to either side of his belt.

After placing more fresh wood upon the fire, Temetet turned to Alonqua. Whatever he was about to say was lost in silence. Friend to friend, brother to brother, they regarded each other as the procession emerged below them. Temetet looked upon the beaded eagle and lightning adorning Alonqua's breechcloth, then lifted his eyes to the eyes of one who was once a boy like himself.

A final clasp of hands and Temetet moved away from his friend, away from the blazing fire, down from the stone ledge, to join his people, whose quiet steps and low voices even now mingled with the faint murmur of flowing water. Alonqua smiled as the brief cry of a baby and the evening song of *chishkukis*, the spring red-breast, met and parted. As Temetet melted into the stone shadows, Alonqua quickly donned his buckskin top, careful of the white feather as he lifted it from beneath the soft hide, and onto his shoulder.

Kishux, the sun, rested a moment on the high ridge. Already evening twilight was rising from the valley floor, while the golden light glistened in the treetops.

"Magic Time," Alonqua whispered, as he looked upon the darkening stones and then up to the sun just now sinking below the western ridge. "Yes, Mawenteh, I remember what you said. 'When *Kishux* touches the Earth, and her light flows across the land, coloring each leaf and blade of grass with a brush of gold—that moment, my son, is Magic Time. It is the moment *Manito* releases light from the upper world, and we feel it enter our hearts.' It is a good time for the People to gather, my old friend."

As his last word met the air he looked down to see the three Clan Mothers emerge from the shadows and ascend the path to the broad terrace just below him. At the center, River-bird Woman carried an unlit torch. To her left strode Beautiful Light holding before her a small earthen pot. To her right, Yellow Moon held a gathering of green cedar fronds. Their pace was slow and stately, befitting their place in the village. When all three arrived at the center of the stone terrace, River-bird Woman turned and raised her free hand.

"*Ala*!"

The shadowy procession trailing down the winding path came to rest. Then there was only the stillness of the evening, no sound, no movement, save the crackling fire high in the shelter, and the whispering brook hidden among the stones below.

Lowering her torch, River-bird Woman turned to one of her partners, Full of Light, and awaited the gift of the ember. As she lifted the lid from a clay bowl, Full of Light held the hot coal to the torch and the single flame bloomed in the evening shadows. In the wavering light, shells brought from the Eastern Sea shimmered upon their long dresses.

Yellow Moon untied her cedar bundle, bent low and scattered the cedar fronds upon the entry path to the stone terrace so that all who walked upon them would be cleared of burdens and protected from hurt.

"*Penteyan Lusi!*"

River-bird Woman's voice, shrill and quavering like a mother Eagle's, echoed and reechoed in the narrow valley. As Alonqua watched, one by one, like glowing beads on a winding thread, the fire-sticks came to life and gathered the scattered hearts. The torch of Pishkwe, Chief Nighthawk, was the last to be lit. Alonqua smiled sadly to see the rugged lines of his face emerge as the flame took hold, the deep-set eyes and white-streaked hair—whiter by far than one would expect of a man in mid-life. His voice was deep, hollow, as if it rose from a stone cave. He held the torch high, spoke the word.

"*Ntanen.*"

The Clan Mothers advanced to the heart of the open place, Mawenteh's grave, then turned and awaited the others. Chief Nighthawk, whose place it was to enter first, instead stood aside for the first feet, those of four village Elders, to cross the soft cedar. All four wore knee-length deerskin robes, two of these trimmed with polished turtle shell, one with wolf fur, one with the feathers of a turkey. Following the Elders, the Warriors, twenty in all, laid down their bows and tomahawks and entered the sacred place. Next came the families, the little ones held or holding close to their mothers, the older ones at more of a distance, as if learning how to walk alone. Just behind, bearing a rolled deerskin and two sticks, the drummer stepped upon and across the cedar. The last to cross, the ten eldest Warriors, lay down their weapons and joined the gathering.

The Chief, who had moved aside to let the others pass, now stepped upon the cedar path and rejoined his people. The circle of hearts enclosing Mawenteh's grave was complete, the string of torches now joining in a glowing necklace.

Until now Alonqua had not moved, perhaps not prepared to

come down from the stone shelter until he had beheld them all, one by one, take their place. As he watched, his eyes filled, then spilled over, and the tears ran down his cheeks and touched the stone. It may be he wept in simple gratitude for their sacred presence, or for loving memories of his days with them, or because they were now so few.

It was time.

As he descended from the fire and came among them, no one spoke, no one embraced him nor took his hand. But each pair of eyes, from the Clan Mothers, to the Elders, to the Chief, to the Warriors, to the baby in her mother's arms, greeted him warmly, with love. And he met the eyes of each with his own eyes as he moved, hand on heart, around the circle. He ended this journey where he began, at the side of the Chief, who placed both hands on Alonqua's shoulders and searched his eyes. The smile which rose on Nighthawk's face was like a new sunrise on a tired land. And Alonqua returned a smile of gratitude toward the only Chief he had had ever known, a man Mawenteh knew well and loved as a brother.

The Chief turned from Alonqua and nodded once to the drummers, one who carried skin and sticks, one who held the tribal drum. Ascending to the shelter each took his place by the fire. The sun's fading embers lingered in the West, while the Silver Moon, two days past half, rose above the trees on the eastern ridge. The chill in the air was softened by the stillness of the night. Chief Nighthawk, holding his torch high, stepped within the ring and stood near the grave of Mawenteh. His deep-set eyes, so often full of sorrow, remained hidden, and as he held his arms out to his People, he summoned his voice to offer the hope and healing his eyes could not.

"*Pentaihemo*! Hear me! All things belong to *Kishelamukong*, the Creator. Your life, your heart, are the gifts of *Kishelamukong*. *Wanishi* to the Maker of each sunrise.

"We offer our thanks to *Manito*, the eternal breath of Creation, the Great Spirit that flows through all things. *Manito*! We ask you to join your breath to ours, to ease our sorrow, hold our hearts, help us to walk the Red Road of Truth until the day we join the River of Stars."

The Chief reached his open hand toward the Great Marsh, and all eyes followed.

"We turn to the East, giver of Spring and new life. To All our Relations to the East, to all who walk the Earth, swim the Waters, soar through the skies—to the trees that rise, to the stones beneath, and the clouds above. I ask your spirits to grace this gathering as we celebrate a man and his spirit and prepare for the new day.

"And to the South, from which flow the Summer winds that nurture our heart's fire, we ask that you release your breath to comfort your children through the hard days to come.

"And to the West, from which our spirits receive the deep heart currents which guide us through our days, we ask you to join your Heart to the rivers of our lifeblood, and give us strength to do what is right.

"And to the North, where dwells the spirit that provides solid Earth and Stone upon which dance the dreams of the Creator, and the cold Winter that prepares the seed for awakening, we ask that you prepare our spirits so that our dreams awaken into true actions."

As Chief Nighthawk and his people closed their eyes in a moment of silence, Alonqua's remained open. He watched their breath-mist rise into the chill air. It may be he recalled the time when his world had broken along with his heart, and Mawenteh entered his life. It may be at this moment, as his eyes looked upon Mawenteh's grave, that he pictured the body placed upon its side, legs drawn up like a baby about to be born from the womb of the Earth. It may be he saw Mawenteh' hand, now lifeless, the hand that had guided him back into the light. Whatever his thoughts, at last Alonqua closed his eyes, and joined his people in silent prayer.

"I will speak few words of this man we call Mawenteh!"

Alonqua's eyes remained closed; one hand moved to the white feather, then to the scar beneath his tunic. Nighthawk found his words, now spoken in a softer voice—less that of a Chief, more just a man.

"We know Mawenteh possessed the wisdom and strength to be chief. He possessed the courage of a warrior, the vision to be Shaman, the memory to be *sachem*, keeper of our story. He chose to be Mawenteh. He chose to be the heart-gatherer in a time when many powers rise to tear us apart. He listened. His few words, his voice and his eyes, steady as a stone, warm as a summer wind, eased our hearts. His presence helped each scattered heart become whole—scattered hearts remain a village."

The chief paused once more, and as his thoughts found the words, the people heard again the voice of a Chief.

"And now we are left to do for ourselves what Mawenteh did for us. We must release this good man's spirit, but hold fast to our memories. I do not wish to darken this gathering with dark thoughts. All here know well the storm that is coming. To remain a Village, to remain a People, to be one whole spirit gathered of many, the best of Mawenteh must now live within us—each one of us. Mawenteh journeys to the stars to do his work. And so we journey here on the earth to do ours. We will travel in darkness. We must watch our feet as we move so that we do not fall. We must pause and rest and look to the stars, so we do not become lost—so we may find our way."

Chief Nighthawk gestured to the flat stone in the center of the circle.

"Any who chooses to place a gift upon his grave may do so now. But Mawenteh asked no gifts remain there, either on the stone, nor buried beneath. It was his wish the gifts be soon retrieved, shared as a remembrance, or offered to the waters of the Great Marsh."

The Chief's eyes turned and found Alonqua. Something close to a smile, a brief shaft of sun through cloud, played on Pishkwe's lips and tired eyes.

"There is one here more able than I to speak of Mawenteh. He has only recently returned to us—and we to him. If it is Alonqua's wish to speak, we would be grateful to hear."

Alonqua did not at once respond, as if he still lived in a dream. It might be he did not hear the words, or simply wished not to speak. The eyes of the village turned to him, waited in silence, all seeing, as Temetet had seen, that something very deep had shifted in the boy they had known. The white feather upon his shoulder was a sign, they knew, of a calling. Eyes still closed, his hand gently tapped the side of his leg, and his chin rose and fell slightly, as if marking the beat of his heart, or a faraway drum none but he could hear.

A night bird, possibly *Ghokos*, the owl, entered the ring of light on silent wings, circled once, and rejoined the dark forest. Alonqua's hand grew still, his head steady. The people watched as he drew in a deep breath, released it slowly, and opened his eyes.

These eyes missed no one, no pair of eyes. It was as if these people were new, and he were new, or that he had known them a long time, but would soon leave them. When at last he looked into the eyes of the Chief, Nighthawk approached him, placed both hands on his shoulders and stepped aside.

His first word was a whisper even he could not hear. The people leaned forward, edged closer. Alonqua turned his eyes to the Moon and Stars, perhaps inviting their soft steady light to enter his heart and offer wisdom.

Ghokos called from the depths of the forest. And then again. Alonqua knew him to be *Chuluhuwe*, the little owl with the voice of a wandering spirit. From across the Valley of Stones flowed the response from another—long, wavering, both yearning and hopeful.

Alonqua turned toward the moon and whispered what none could hear.

"She is calling you, *Chuluhuwe*, It is time you join her, as I have joined my people. It is not good to be alone too long."

Beneath the stars, amid the stones, with shining eyes he traced the jewels of the glowing ring.

And then he spoke the words his heart had uncovered.

CHAPTER 14

DRUMS, HEARTS, WINGS

"My people—when the moon was young, Mawenteh sent me on a journey into the rain.

"As I traveled I talked with trees and animals. One time I talked with a star. I think they listened.

I came here and I talked with Temetet. He is my friend so at least he pretended to listen."

"You who have gathered here are not *Kwenoomuk*, not *Temakwe*. You are not *Xaxakwe*, the Tree that has healed. You are not Temetet, a friend who is only a boy like me. With them I am not afraid to speak and the words come.

"Now Chief Nighthawk asks if I have words for you. My first thought is to hide. There are many of you and only one of me. And I am young to speak to so many who have the wisdom of many years."

"But I have a voice. My love for Mawenteh—and for you—move my heart to speak."

Alonqua raised his eyes from the people to the stars.

"*Gitchi Manito— Kishelamukong!* You have blessed this night, this gathering—this man we called Mawenteh. *Wanishi*!"

His words, like shy forest animals from hidden dens, emerged slowly, with great care.

"There is none here—whose heart he did not touch—awaken—and guide—in a quiet and secret way—he gathered each of our hearts—helped each to find its own truth. I saw the same man you saw—it might be I saw a little more. We shared adventures. He listened to me—closely—no matter how foolish my words. He...he…"

Alonqua's eyes opened wide and he smiled.

"Yes—yes—Mawenteh taught me *how* to learn—never what. If I had a question—he showed me how to find the answer—myself. Answers that are real and true, he said, take time. 'Look to the animals,' he said. 'Watch them a long time. Learn from them. Watch the trees in the wind, on still days—watch them rest in winter *and* greet the sun in spring with fresh leaves. Watch the clouds, the stars—watch the flow of water—hear its music and its words.

"Mawenteh sheltered me when I believed in nothing—when I had no one. Mawenteh's kindness—his love—was like the sun. Day by day, my heart opened again. And for every hurt, there came a moment of wonder.

"There is something else—a spirit seed he planted in my heart. I have no words for this—only the visions of a Healing Tree—and a black stick deep within a nest."

He shook his head and stepped back.

"No! Forgive me—I am speaking of myself to myself—I will try to speak for him now—to you."

The white feather upon his shoulder trembled as a cool breeze flowed down the ridge. Alonqua reached across to touch it.

"Mawenteh is here. His spirit is here. His journey to the River of Stars—is not now. He is here. This is what he wants you to know. Do not look. You will not see him. Do not listen. You will not hear his voice. I do not know what calling holds his spirit here. I do not know how long he will stay. But if his presence—knowing he is here—once more gathers hearts that are breaking—that is a good thing."

Alonqua looked to the chief.

"Chief Nighthawk, as ever, spoke truth when he said we must keep the truth of Mawenteh in our hearts. Hard days have come. We are fewer. Too few to wage battle. We feel the cold fingers that touch our hearts each dawn.

"Mawenteh sent me out into the night to find my way. That journey is not over. Our journey into the dark begins. It will be soon.

"But know this. One night Mawenteh and I shared a fire near the river. My heart was boiling like the pot of stew on the flames. With words bitter as willow bark, I asked him if the hurt would ever cease—mine, and the hurt we all know. I asked what will stop the salt-eaters from taking our lands, our way of life, our lives. I asked if even our stories would die and all would pass away like a dying fire in the night.

"This is what he said to me—and now to you. Hold his words close—take the meaning into your heart. 'Whatever is true and right will never die, but like a wave on the water, move ever onward until it reaches the shore.'"

As Alonqua lowered his head the evening wind rose again, and the still leafless trees sighed beneath the golden moon.

Alonqua looked to River-bird Woman, alone in her island of torchlight, her eyes turned inward, mourning her husband. As Alonqua came to her, he stood and held out his arms. The little woman looked up; her eyes, turned outward now, met his. For the first time in days she smiled. She reached out and drew him to her. They did not weep. They simply held on.

"I am grateful you have come home, Alonqua. Seeing you well is a great blessing."

Alonqua smiled at her words, at the reedy voice he knew so well. He looked into her old eyes, alive now and full of stars.

"And it is my blessing to see you, River-bird Woman."

A long wavering call sounded from the forest edge.

"Do you think Mawenteh is the owl calling us?"

"No, Alonqua, I do not think so. But you know his ways. No doubt he persuaded the old bird to be his messenger. Mawenteh wishes us to know that he is near, that he is well, that he sees us here together under the River of Stars."

"Chosen Mother, I see a kettle has been placed above the fire, and that the water is already steaming. Will the Clan Mothers join me at the fire? I have a gift for the Village."

Alonqua waited until the three elder women gathered. Arm-in-arm they made their way up the steep path to the stone shelter. Alonqua followed close, holding out his arms in respect and protection should they fall. But their steps were sure and soon all four stood between fire and stone.

Alonqua reached into a niche in the wall and placed the roots in the hands of River-bird Woman, who lifted them beneath her nose and breathed deep.

"*Xaxakwe!* And such a gift, Alonqua!"

"You know what Mawenteh would say—these are the Tree's gift, not mine, freely offered to me just before the great storm struck, as the war shouts of *Pethakuwe* thundered down the valley."

"The roots hold power Alonqua. I feel it in my fingers. This is a good thing. *Wanishi* to *Xaxakwe*. *Wanishi* to you who gathered the gift."

River-bird Woman handed a third of the roots to Beautiful Light, another third to Yellow Moon, and together the Clan Mothers released the roots, one by one, into the steaming water.

The drums came to life, first the low, booming heartbeat of the tribal drum, then the high staccato of the skin-beater striking the rigid hide. Alonqua and the Clan Mothers returned to the broad terrace. Many hands touched his as his People moved past him on their way to leave gifts for Mawenteh.

When all had passed, when each gift had been placed upon the flat stone, Alonqua looked to the moon once more, now swimming through thin clouds.

"I have nothing to offer you, my friend—only my love. I trust that is enough."

The People gathered again, this time in an arc at the far edge of the open place. The drum and hide came together and caught a fierce rhythm which all knew well as the drum song of the Thunder-Beings. Sticks gripped with hands a-blur cracked upon the stiff hide like the lightning crackling from the talons. The answering deep beats gave voice to the thunder, *Pethakuwe's* war cries.

Two of the Warriors ascended to the fire, slid a stout pole through the handle of the iron kettle, and carried the storm-gathered gift to the center of the terrace. Three village Elders approached the kettle, each holding a large drinking gourd which they placed in the hands of the clan mothers. In turn, each dipped her gourd into the amber-colored gift.

River-bird Woman turned from the fire and to her people. Holding the dripping gourd close to her heart, she closed her eyes and spoke.

"What *Wanikwe* offers is her own precious roots who hold the power of the Thunder-Beings. The roots were gathered under a shaking sky. *Pethakuwe's* power entered the tree—branches to trunk—trunk to roots. Now this power rests in my hands, in the hands of my sisters. Great Spirit, as all share this sacred gift, we ask its power to restore our wounded spirits, and lift our eyes to the shining stars."

Turning to the gathered families, River-bird Woman addressed the children.

"Young Ones, you will taste first, as it must always be. You see this earth with new eyes. You hear our stories with new ears. It is you who will carry our dreams and give them life."

The littlest ones, still in their mother's arms, tasted warm drops from the old woman's finger. The other children, wide-eyed with wonder, sipped from the offered gourd.

"Now to the mothers, from whom these children came to life, may *Wa's* gift enter your hearts so that love and courage join in sacred dance,"

One by one, the women approached the gourd and drank. River-bird Woman turned and walked to the kettle to join her sisters. Yellow Sun held her gourd, extending it to the silent men.

"To you, the Warriors, the good men who hunt and protect, The Thunder Tree offers you the power to be watchful, to be strong in your heart, to be faithful in your every act for the good of your people."

After each man had received his portion she returned to the kettle, still steaming in the torchlight.

Beautiful Light passed her gourd to Yellow Moon, who drank and passed it on to River-bird Woman, who, as she touched her lips to the warm brew, gave thanks to Alonqua with her eyes.

Placing the drinking gourd back in Beautiful Light's hand,

she turned to the Elders and Chief.

"To those we look to for the wisdom born of years, may you find strength and wisdom in these roots to be the roots of our people, no matter where our feet take us."

Each of the Elders drank in turn, lowered his head and passed the gourd—until it reached the chief. He tipped the gourd, held the sacred brew a moment behind tight lips, and slowly swallowed. He tipped the gourd and the remaining drops touched the earth.

"*Wanishi, Wanikwe.* Your gift is now part of us. *Wanishi*, Alonqua, for gathering the storm-root, whose spirit we receive with gratitude,"

Chief Nighthawk dipped the gourd deep in the kettle and held it out to Alonqua, Holding the brimming vessel, he paused as the drumming grew louder, more intense.

"No more words," whispered Alonqua. "The Thunder-Beings—it is time."

He held the gourd high, as if to touch the stars, and then he drank deep. What was left he flung upwards, golden drops touched by torchlight. Kneeling, he placed one hand upon the White Feather, the other upon the Earth, and lifted his eyes to the stars.

Just above Alonqua, on either side of the fire, the drums now slowed once again to the rhythm of a human heart. The circle of torches tightened as he took his place at its center. He spread out his arms, bowed to the Earth, rose and faced the Four Directions. The drummers struck, harder, faster, as the beat meshed with the storm in his heart. Turning and turning, knees high, feet stabbing the Earth with each thunder beat, his dance became a living thing. He reached high to touch the stars, lowered them to his sides, raised them level, then up, down, up. He bent his elbows slightly, and moved his arms with the grace and power of a bird of prey. The drum grew fierce as his pace quickened, and he danced with the beat, ever faster, arms pumping, knees high, stone-dust rising, body twisting, stretching, yearning.

In the flickering torchlight the dance shifted to a grim struggle. Alonqua's eyes beckoned the stars, but his body remained tied to the Earth. And he was tiring. His arms, his legs lost the rhythm, grew frantic. Beads of sweat gathered, rolled down to join his tears.

The end drew near.

"*Newichema*! Help him!"

Through his pain and yearning, Alonqiua heard her, River-bird Woman. She came to him and held out her hands. Beautiful Light held one and Yellow Moon clasped the other, and then joined each other's. Within their tight circle of power, Alonqua grew still. He looked with wonder into the eyes of each. Someday he would speak of this moment. He would say their years had fallen away, and they were young and strong, with raven hair and flashing eyes. He would speak of their goddess power, and of their joining their hearts with his own. What is known by all who were there is that the Clan Mothers joined hands around a weary boy—and began to dance.

They danced a dance of timeless dignity, solemn, slow, two steps and a pause—two steps and a pause—around and around, their eyes ever on the white feather bound by the red cord.

Then, as one, the village rose, each man, woman and child, and formed yet another ring of power. They matched their steps to the pounding drums, bowing, rising, as they circled the Clan Mothers. From the stones themselves, rose the deeper thunder of ancient drums, like the beat of the heart of the Earth. And from the Sky rose a wind. The air poured in from all directions, spinning, whirling, pulsing—living.

The two heart-rings spun faster and the wind followed, lifting dead leaves, sticks, and sand and spiraling them toward the stars. At the center, at the still core of the wind, a boy felt a trembling touch upon his ear like the stroke of a butterfly wing or the touch of a white feather, now rising from his shoulder. Closing his eyes, Alonqua spread his arms, bowed low, touched the Earth, rose and reached for the sky. Again—again—again.

And then, "*Yukwe*!" is what the People heard.

Now!

And he was free.

CHAPTER 15
SKY JOURNEY

The stunning jolt from fear to freedom struck his heart like an arrow of cleansing fire. And freedom was a pathless path through a world of sky. His feet were talons rooted in the living air. At his side moved not arms but wings with long feathers dark as the night.

The rising air lifted and turned him in tight spirals, as a leaf in an autumn storm. Above the treetops the updraft faltered, and his frantic wingbeats were the flailing arms of a drowning man.

He looked down to the earth rising to meet him, and in a frozen moment, joined his eyes, first one then the other, to those of River-bird Woman. Unlike the rest of his people, who still watched the dark dancer at the center, she had cast her eyes upward to follow his spirit, as did each child.

Her eyes spoke of trust—the children, of wonder. Both called to his heart, and then there was one powerful wingbeat, then another, even stronger, then another. Once again, he rose clear of the trees. Once again, he looked down to the glowing rings, now still, as if frozen in a cave of ice. From the night mist emerged a wonder. Around the torch-rings wraithlike dancers took form, glowing dancers writhing and twisting like flames in the wind, dark hair floating, hollow eyes turned upward. With newborn eyes, Sapelei Opalanie, Shining Eagle, watched the light gather in in the dark sockets, watched as the eyes of The Old Ones shone like those of the children. They had come to honor

Mawenteh—and to free the Eagle Spirit rising to the stars.

Alonqua cried out but found no words of thanks. Shining Eagle called to all those below as he soared in ever widening, ever rising spirals above the Valley of Stones. Each wingbeat, measured and slow, pushed him higher until the rings of light were a flickering star in a sea of darkness. He wheeled toward the Great Marsh as the half-moon poured down its light, silvering the new ice along the shallows. His hungry eyes were keen to be fed and so his wings, strong now and sure, carried him down, down toward the shimmering marsh where his moon shadow sent a raft of ducks scattering for shelter in a shower of spray. On wooded islands he saw the tiny birds huddled in clefts of trees, a mouse emerging from a reed nest, daubs of blood on the muzzle of a fox carrying to her den a limp rabbit.

He clenched his talons as a fish rose and shattered the floating moon, but the Eagle turned away, answering a greater call. Then the lodge of *Temakwe* passed beneath him, and he once more crossed the heart of the marsh to the Sacred Place—the great stone, *Ahsen*, and the silver moon-spray of *Sukpehelak.* Banking his wings, he veered toward the desolate *Aptachuteh,* then soared low, just above ancient tree-bones thrusting up from the black water. Ahead was the Island of Light, shimmering under the stars, anchored by the tree of life with its patches of ivory bark glistening in the moonlight.

Opalanie lingered at the place of *Kwenoomuk*'s pain. He turned to the shallow channel, where an unknown friend had saved his life. And when he soared once more above the lodge of *Temakwe* and saw his harbor of safety, he turned his eyes up the shoreline to a point of land. His wings faltered as he neared the ancient tree, charred and split by the arrow of fire, the nest ruin scattered below.

He had nowhere left to fly, nowhere but toward the stars. But as his wings took him higher, the stars withdrew behind a veil of cloud. One by one they were lost, and he flew more swiftly, chasing the few that remained. And then there was just one star, tucked far away in a clear pocket of sky, just above the far edge of the Earth.

I know you, whispered the Star, *and have waited for you.*

The Eagle paused, then pursued the fading star. "And I know you, my friend, though you have changed."

No, not I. It is you, Sapelei Opalanie, who have changed, not your heart, but your eyes. Use them well, for they are a great gift.

"My ever-shining friend and now my guide, show me the way."

That I will do. But on this journey prepare yourself for the Great Mystery.

So Shining Eagle flew on into the night, in pursuit of the ever-distant star that inspired every wingbeat. At first he saw only the star, but then between the star and the dark horizon, a sudden light shimmered across the sky and was gone. Another pulse of light, closer now, revealed a heaving cloud-mountain rise from the Earth like *Pamputis* from his lair.

Sapelei Opalanie looked for the Star, but its light had been swallowed by the darkness. Only its voice remained, so distant only his heart could hear.

Our paths part here. Here is the storm you seek. This storm knows you, has touched you, waited for you, and calls for you. Should you emerge from the fury, should your own heart still beat, look for me, and I will guide you home.

"*Wanishi*, my friend. I will look for you."

With no earth to stand upon, no tree to anchor him, nothing but wings to support him, he pierced the shell of a storm seething with turbulent darkness and shattering light. No shelter here. None. Wind-blasted, rain-beaten, thunder-shaken, his wings faltered as he fought to find the storm's heart. The storm, as if enraged at so bold a trespass, raked him with hailstones, sought him out with arrows of white fire. He shouted out, not to defy nor surrender, and the storm heard the call of a sky-horse, the shrill cry of an eagle.

Just as the boy, in the heart of a raging storm, joined the power, Shining Eagle gathered his heart and flew with the winds, inviting them to carry him, and looking to the lightning to light his path. The angry winds again tore at him, but he turned with them. The storm spears lit up the boiling clouds, and he watched their edges tear away and spin upwards. A cold wind poured down from icy cloud tops and drove him down, down, until his wings caught calmer air and pulled him free. Clawing at the storm-wind with feather and talon he burst into the turbulent column of rising vapor, and with power ebbing with each heartbeat, he drove his wings and pierced the spinning wall of wind and soared into the great heart of the living storm.

At once the turbulent air grew calmer, warmer, rain-sweetened, rising like a blessing from the heart of the Earth. He spread his wings wide and was carried upward in wide spiraling rings.

As he soared higher and higher the supporting winds grew colder, stranger. The smell of Earth faded and the rain froze in tiny pellets, as both he and the ice still rose toward the luminous crown of the storm. Yet higher the upward breath of the storm ceased. The eagle flailed his wings and found them stiff and heavy with a layer of frost. At the very peak of the clouds icy orbs, too heavy to rise further, hovered for an instant, spinning and glistening in the pulsing light of fire spears far below.

One by one the ice-stones paused, then fell, disappearing in the storm-mist. He watched them tumble toward the only world he had ever known. He looked down, but he did not follow. Instead he turned his eyes upward and flew higher. The thin air was laced with frozen mist, and his lungs throbbed with the pain of taking it in. And then the mist dissolved. Above him were the stars, suspended like countless jewels across the heavens. Below him was the storm, seething and churning like an angry bear. Somewhere below the storm was the Earth, his home, and all that he had ever loved.

In the cold, under the stars, wings heavy, covered with glittering ice, Shining Eagle turned his eyes upward and saw the little star.

"Not yet, my friend!" his heart cried as he angled his wings and traveled down the far edge of the storm's heart.

Soon the air warmed and the ice still clinging to his wings melted away. Having found the stars, he sought the lightning. Each jagged strike lit the clouds, freezing them into fantastic shapes; each spear of white fire drew him closer and closer to its source. The answering thunder struck him like blows from a war club, and the air itself seemed to seethe and burn. Had he not the eyes of an Eagle the next spear of fire would have blinded him. Instead his eyes received the light. And the light revealed the *Pethakuwe.*

He was the warrior of the sky-battle, a shining Eagle of unspeakable size, feathers ablaze, trailing sparks as from a wind-torn fire. From his gnarled feet and curved talons burst yet another jagged spear of fire. The great hooked beak, blood-red, opened, and the war shout shook the skies. The burning wings rose, then fell, and the wind tumbled him over and over. Righting himself, Sapelei Opalanie, turned back in time to see one more white spear explode from the talons. In that instant the flaming yellow eye of the Thunder-Being looked into his own. Then he was gone, swallowed by the same battle he was waging. Though he could not see the others, he was not alone, as across the sky the fire-spears rained down, and the thunder shook the heavens.

The *Pethakuwe* pushed the storm swiftly onward, until all that remained were the pulses of distant light and the low rumble of fading war shouts. The star was waiting. He had kept his word, as all stars do.

I am thankful you live.

"And I am thankful you are here, my friend. I am tired. And I need to be home."

That does not surprise me, not at all. Here you will not need my light. Look down and see the river you have traveled many times.

"How can this be? I flew too far to be so close."

Your friend must have said to you that the journey to face one's fears is far longer and harder than the journey home. And here is a question for you—how can a boy be an eagle? Trust the Great Mystery, Sapelei Opalanie. Trust your spirit.

The moon shone once more and Shining Eagle soared beneath its light like some forgotten spirit of the night. Below, a river alive with rippling stars pointed the way home.

CHAPTER 16
KISHELAMUKONG

Alonqua awakened to a throbbing pain in his shoulders. He opened his eyes to the half moon, strangely distant like the memory of a long-absent friend. Then a face eclipsed the moon, lit by firelight, framed by stars. A warm hand slid beneath his head and raised it from the cold stone.

In her other hand River-bird Woman cradled a white feather. "Alonqua, this feather carried you away, and now it brings you home. It must have great power. The moment your sky-dance ceased this fell from you, and a breath of air brought it to me."

Alonqua struggled to rise, then lay back again. River-bird Woman offered him the gift and his trembling hand received it.

"When I touched the feather it was cold as ice. Alonqua, my brave son—where did you fly?"

He sat up and shook his head. His voice was a whisper only she could hear.

"To the stars—nearly to the stars. It was cold there, River-bird Woman—and beautiful. I am thankful to have come so close. But I am grateful to be here, to be close to you and the people."

"Alonqua, your spirit rose as an Eagle. The children saw. I watched their eyes rise to the stars. And then you were gone, all but your earth-form. Your body danced as the moon rose high, never pausing, never tiring, on and on. The people watched in wonder, urged you on. And when the drummers tired and laid down their sticks to rest the people carried the beat, feet on stone, stone on stone, stick on stick."

She looked upon Alonqua with eyes shining. As he sat up she took his hand and held it tight.

"And then I heard the children speak your name. One by one they looked up and pointed to the sky, their eyes filled with wonder!"

River-bird Woman reached for Alonqua's free hand and into it she placed the white feather.

"Alonqua, as you danced, as you flew, did you hear thunder? Not from our drums, my son, but from the sky?"

"Yes, good Mother. I heard thunder—felt a great wind, tasted rain. I saw the *Pethakuwe*—his wings of fire, his shining eyes. River-bird Woman, he turned those eyes on me."

"Do not speak of this, Alonqua. Not now. One cannot speak a dream before he wakes, and your dream is truer than even these old stones, which even now are melting away winter by winter. Your dream is a gift, and you are the one who carries the gift from the Spirit World to the Earth. That is what Eagles do. The dream goes on, and Sapelei Opalanie will live that dream until it gives way to another."

Her smile spoke of joy and sorrow. Before Alonqua could speak, she placed her hand beneath his buckskin top and touched the scar.

"You wonder how I know your spirit name? My son, old women can dream as well. As you fell from the sky and lay upon the Earth, I searched for the sign that my dream was true. The scar..."

Alonqua looked past her face to the moon that once seemed so close. Then he sat up and searched her face, her eyes, as if for the first time.

"It is no wonder Mawenteh chose you as his wife."

"Alonqua, my son, we chose each other."

"Yes! Yes—that is how it must be—I should have…"

Touching her finger to her lips, River-bird Woman turned her eyes to her fellow Clan Mothers, then to the Elders and to the Chief, then to the Warriors and to the families. All had waited in silence. All had granted this pair the sacred space to share their hearts.

"Say not another word, Alonqua. I know your heart better than you know your own. We will speak more. But now you need rest. The chief will wish to speak with you, but I will say to him this is not the time."

She rose and took both of his hands. "Rest here, my son. The Village is not your place tonight. It is still too soon. I will leave you another blanket and a fur."

"*Wanishi*, River-bird Woman. I will rest here, hold vigil here, recalling my seasons with Mawenteh. May his spirit and your memories comfort you. Rest well. At the rising of the sun I follow my heart and join the Village."

She released his hands and approached the Chief. A few words and a slow shake of the head was enough. Chief Nighthawk looked past her to the one who had only days ago been a boy. He nodded to Alonqua, placed his hand on his heart, and motioned to the drummers. The rhythm began as a slow heartbeat—two beats and a pause—two beats and a pause.

Alonqua smiled. He knew the chant the drums were preparing, and also knew Mawenteh would approve. The Chant of the Creator was no death song, no funeral chant. This was a song for the living, a song of faith, of growth, of moving forward. It was a song of Spring.

Alonqua was aware that all eyes were on him, and that as the drumbeats echoed in the valley, all awaited his voice. In their eyes he saw love and the hope that his journey offered them hope in a hopeless time. They needed him now. They needed to hear his voice lifted in song. And so he rose from the side of River-bird Woman and looked up to the stars he had almost touched. In a voice clear and strong, he began—

"*Kishelamukong... Kishelamukong...*

Kishelamukong... Kishelamukong...

A-weh, a-weh, a-weh...A-weh, a-weh, a-weh..."

He paused and turned to the Clan Mothers. It was Mawenteh's wife who sang first, her voice high and quavering like the call of a riverbird lost above the clouds.

"Kishelamukong... Kishelamukong...
Kishelamukong... Kishelamukong...
A-weh, a-weh, a-weh...A-weh, a-weh, a-weh..."

Then the other elder women joined, like a sudden wave, voices old and strong, splitting the darkness and rising to the stars. And as the Elders joined, followed by Warriors, then mothers, fathers, and children, the stars bent low and listened.

A good man had passed, and a village which had mourned his death now sang of gratitude for his life, all life, with a chant whose rhythms were old as the Earth. The song went on and on, became a living thing, hovered among the timeless stones beneath a golden moon.

Then the drums stopped and there were only the voices. The Warriors lit fresh torches and handed a few to each group within the gathering. The families were first to still their voices and depart, followed by the Warriors, the Chief and the Elders. Last was River-bird Woman, her old voice one with the voice of Alonqua, the voice of a young man who had returned with another name that none but she would ever know. And in her eyes he saw that she knew his heart, knew of his spirit journey, saw her faith that he was strong enough to carry the burden.

"Kishelamukong... Kishelamukong...
Kishelamukong... Kishelamukong...
A-weh, a-weh, a-weh...A-weh, a-weh, a-weh..."

Both voices trailed off into the night. Both pairs of arms held each other and then let go. Alonqua offered River-bird Woman a torch, but she shook her head. In the firelight he saw her smile.

"No, Alonqua. I know the way, even in the darkness."

Then she was gone.

Alonqua climbed to the ledge above the stone shelter. From there his eyes followed the bobbing lights of guiding torches weaving their way toward the village until the last was swallowed by the forest.

The night called to him with the voice of silence. The fading fire called as well, and so he rose and returned to the softly glowing flames. He fed the fire once more, then made his way down the steep trail to Mawenteh's burial place. Upon reaching the stone slab, Alonqua leaned his torch over the many cherished objects placed upon it. Each gift felt his touch; some he cradled in his hand as though they held life. A crystal of blood-red garnet felt warm in his palm. The feather of a sparrow quivered in the still air. Old eyes looked into his from a weathered stone. There was one more he held, a split and hollow cocoon.

Raising the empty house to the torchlight, Alonqua found it to be dark-brown, constructed of overlapping chestnut leaves. He slipped his thumb past the opening and felt the silk lining, one long strand spun round and round within the drawn-in leaves. The silk-spinner was gone—not just gone, but changed from fat leaf-eater to what Mawenteh liked to call the moon-flier, whose ghostly green wings Alonqua saw often fluttering above summer campfires.

"Who left this gift?" he asked. "Was it an old man soon to leave this world? Was it offered by a child who has only just joined it?"

Alonqua turned his eyes away from the hollow shell and lifted them to the moon.

"Where are you, Mawenteh?" he whispered. "Your empty shell lies beneath this stone. Where have your wings taken you? Or do you hover very near? Can you touch my shoulder? Once? To help me gather my heart as you have done so many times?"

His answer came not with a touch, but with a sound so faint that it might have recalled slow waves of gentle rain on a distant forest. Alonqua looked to the star-filled sky, then down to the moon-silvered stones. Placing the cocoon upon the stone he slowly rose and spoke to the night.

"Kishelamukong! I hear your breath! All around—above—below. Slowly, so slowly! In—out—in again—out once more. It is the breath of the night. It is the breath of creation. It is the breath of my friend released to join the breath of the trees, the animals, the stones, the stars!"

Alonqua bowed his head and held out his arms. And as the moon reached the peak of the sky, he joined his breath with his Creator.

Above, in the stone shelter, a dying fire awaited new life.

Chapter 17

DARK MESSAGE

In the soft gray light of a cold dawn, cradled between two stones, Alonqua opened his eyes

He rose to stir the embers and then laid on fresh wood. As the flames rose, he watched fingers of mist drift down the narrow valley on their way to the river far below. Near the banks of the river a village was awakening. His quiet night alone had passed and it was time to join them.

Before departing the Valley of Stones and the grave of Mawenteh, he knelt and opened his medicine pouch. He held the feather to his heart, then bound it to the red cord of his father.

The path he chose to the village was not the one his people had walked on their night journey home. Alonqua's path, one favored by wary deer, moved upward along the valley side, over the rocky ridge, and down to a broad shelf of land. There, well above spring floods, yet an arrow's flight from the river, lay his village. When Alonqua reached the high ridgetop, he sat upon a log and looked down to plumes of smoke rising from *wikewams* and Lodge House.

"Mawenteh, my friend," he whispered, "When my father went to war seven winters ago, I remember counting the dwellings seven times on the fingers of both hands. Fewer than half remain. The old ones die. The little ones do not thrive. The young men are leaving, some to fight, some to join the whites. The winter has been long. Food caches are low. There is little meat to mix with the cornmeal boiling in the iron kettles."

Alonqua rose and looked South toward the Great Marsh.

"What are they to do, Mawenteh? What am I to do?"

Just as he began to move down the ridge and toward the village far below, a movement along the river trail caught his eye. A lone runner emerged from the river mist. Reaching the village, he strode swiftly to the council lodge. After a brief hearing, Chief Nighthawk motioned him to the entrance and summoned the elders to join him in the council lodge.

Alonqua lingered above the village, content to let the runner's news be heard. Only when he saw the gathered families disperse to their homes and three warriors emerge from the Council Lodge did he rise and make his way down the steep slope. Halfway to the village he froze at the sudden yipping of the dogs. The runner had arrived not far ahead of another man. Alonqua looked north along the along river path and saw him, a tall man moving swiftly with long sure strides. In one hand he held a musket, in the other a leather satchel. The warriors, one armed with a musket, two with tomahawks, awaited him where the path entered the village.

Alonqua moved closer, and as the tall man came to a halt, studied his face. Even at this distance it was plain this man held no fear nor defiance, neither in posture nor expression.

There at the edge of the village, a mere arm-length from the warriors, he lay down his gun, removed his broad-brimmed hat, and raised his hand as the sign of peace. Offering the satchel to the man closest, he pointed to the lodge and made the sign for "Chief."

One warrior took his place on one side, one on the other, one behind, and as they proceeded to the Council Lodge. Alonqua, as yet unseen, followed from a distance. His sudden appearance ignited neither surprise nor special greeting from those who had chosen to gather near the lodge. As if expecting him, they silently parted to provide a path to enter. His place within the village had changed. Perhaps it had to do with deep respect for Mawenteh. Perhaps it was Alonqua, himself, and what they had seen in his eyes after he returned from the stars.

The reason was of no concern to Alonqua, who acknowledged his people with a faint smile and a nod, and then entered the lodge. The air within was chill, though warming to the crackle of flames freshly fed. The eldest of the elders, now that Mawenteh was gone, had urged the coals of the council fire to new life. Mawenteh had told Alonqua often that in the sixty winters since he had come to this valley as a young man, the fire had never been neglected, had never died. And so this fire, hot and new, had been rekindled, and in its warmth the Chief received the gift of tobacco from one who was now guest and awaited his words.

Alonqua stood to one side, a little in the shadows. He looked hard at this man who had come among them, and waited to hear the voice that would speak words that matched the eyes. The Chief, aware of Alonqua's presence, approached him, placed his hand on his shoulder, and turned to the guest.

"This is Alonqua. We rejoice he is here. As you see he is young in winters, but in his heart you will see the man who, *Manito* willing, may someday lead us. Now please, my friend, tell us what you have come so far to say."

The tall man did not at once speak. His eyes were fixed upon Alonqua whose eyes were fixed upon his. Then he turned from Alonqua, pointed to the east, and spoke the single word.

"Solchelak!"

Soldiers! The word cut the air and pierced the hearts of all who heard it. The man extended his hand and moved it to his chest.

"Iheh...."

He spoke haltingly, but his words were clear and true. Few whites would know this word, as it was seldom spoken even by the Lenape. *"Iheh"* did not simply mean "coming" but was reserved for the approach of a great tragedy, like a great storm, or a long winter with no food. The chief's eyes hardened. The silence in the lodge hung like frost in the air.

The man took a sip from the water gourd, cleared his throat and spoke.

"Kweti Kishku...."

One day—only one—and the soldiers would reach the village. Two more words followed quickly, "*Utenenet....lusi....*"

No one breathed. No one moved.

"Solchchelak iheh kweti kishku utenenet lusi." The tall man did not have to speak these dreaded words in Lenape. He could have said in plain English that the soldiers would arrive in one day to burn the village. He would have been understood. All but the little ones knew some English. It was not lost on those present that the man who had come to warn them chose to use Lenape out of respect. And it was out of respect for this man that the Chief chose English words in response.

"Yours is a spirit both brave and kind to travel far and allow us time to gather our hearts and leave this valley. We have known for some time this was coming. Since the death of the war chief, Tecumseh, we knew no treaty would save us. We have heard of villages to the South and East burned, many with no warning, people fleeing for their lives even as the smoke was rising. We had thought another summer, perhaps two, good harvests, growing stronger, preparing, sending scouts to search another home."

Chief Nighthawk brought a few sticks to the fire and looked upon the elders and turned to Alonqua.

"You, my son, whose eyes tell me you have journeyed to the stars. What did you see that can help us now? What did you find that can offer us hope?"

Alonqua raised his eyes to the Chief and shook his head.

"I wish I could give what you ask. I have no answer for you, for the People, for myself—not now. What I saw, what I found, I do not understand. It is too soon—. I regret this with all my heart."

"No Alonqua, it is I who regret. I ask out of weakness, to remove my burden by placing it on you. Forgive me if you can."

"Chief Nighthawk, there is nothing to forgive. Nothing. You seek to help the village. You asked what any good man would ask. My journey may serve us all someday, though it offers us nothing that will stop or ease what is to come. This I regret. But I had not finished. There is more to say, and it has to do with light—and hope—for all of us."

"What is this hope, my son! Your eyes shine with it and we would wish to know it."

Turning his eyes from the Chief, Alonqua looked into the eyes of the tall man. Their hands met, clasped, and held on.

"This man, this good man—he is the hope. This man who has come so far to help us. Just days ago, at the edge of the Great Marsh, this man saved my life."

The silence in the lodge was broken only by the crackling fire. No one moved. No one spoke. But all eyes were on the tall man at the center of the lodge.

"And now," said Alonqua, "you know why I have hope—not that the soldiers will turn back and that we can live on in this home—but hope that there will be a time, maybe not in your lifetime, or mine, when there will be peace and healing. Mawenteh spoke truth—'what is true and right will never die.' That this man is here—that I am alive—joins the wave of truth that will surely 'reach the shore.'"

He turned to the Chief. For the first time in many moons Alonqua saw light in his weary eyes.

"Chief Nighthawk, I ask you grant me a short time alone with our guest. I would speak with him before he leaves the village. Please share with the people all that I have said. Say that I will soon tell the story of my rescue from death, and that this man is the sign of better days. Only a short time—and I will join you."

The Chief nodded, and as he and the elders rose to leave the lodge, each took a stick and placed it upon the fire and clasped the hand of the tall man who had saved one life, perhaps many more. . When all had departed, Alonqua looked up into the eyes of a mystery.

"I know you are called Joshua. I heard your name spoken—I see from your eyes you remember me. You, who have saved me from the angry hands of your people—are here to warn my people of great danger. Both are great risks for you—why?"

Joshua looked away and shook his head.

"Alonqua, I think it better you do not know my reason. You

and your people might not think so highly of me."

"I will not ask again. Someday you may choose to tell me, but that will be your concern. But know there is nothing you could say that would change the truth that we are brothers, not of blood, but of the heart."

"I hope that is true. No one can know how much I hope that is true"

"It is true. You will see."

"Alonqua, it is past time for me to leave. Convey my best hopes for your village. *Weli Kishku,* my friend. You have old eyes for one so young."

Alonqua smiled, once more extending his hand.

"And a good day to you as well, Joshua. You have kind eyes for one so white!"

Returning the smile, Joshua made the clasp, then walked past Alonqua and into the light of day. Just before he reached the edge of the village he turned and held his hand high.

"May God—may *Manito*—be with you all!" he shouted.

Alonqua watched him move up the river path and fade into the forest.

"And with you," he whispered.

Chapter 18

TORN HEARTS

The late morning silence was broken by a sound unlike any Alonqua had ever heard. It was the unforgiving sound of iron on stone. First one—then two—then from the heart of the village the strikes increased, grew louder. With his ears he heard the force behind each heavy blow. With his heart he felt the sorrow and the anger. The *wikewam* at the village edge shielded his eyes from the source, so he moved toward the sound until at last he saw.

The women had not waited to hear of the White Man's warning. They knew. All too well.

They had retrieved their iron kettles from each of their homes and had gathered around the large stone which lay at the heart of the village. And now, with no words spoken, mouths grimly set, one after another, each woman raised the heavy iron and heaved it upon the rock.

The striking of iron on stone, again and again and again, on and on, awakened a sorrow Alonqua had never known. He looked at the eyes of the women, and they were hard like the stone. They had cooked many meals in these kettles, but they were too heavy for long travels. And they were made by the people who would burn their village. Some of the elder women had kept clay pots, and knew how to make them. The old ways have their place in times of change.

The women heaved the kettles so that the same spot would strike the stone each time. Soon the dull ringing changed pitch as the weakened place cracked, gave way, splitting the brittle iron on the enduring stone. Each woman, as her pot cracked open, stood in her place and waited for the others to finish. There was sorrow in their eyes, and anger. There were no tears.

The blows grew fewer and fewer until, at last, there remained only broken shells. The clouds had gathered, and once again the sound of rain settled upon the village, no longer the sweet rain of dawn. Alonqua stood with the women, shared this moment with them, struggled to share their hearts and soften their hurt. He knew he could do no more than this—nor less. One by one their eyes met his, and he knew they were grateful for his presence, there in the very heart of the dying village, under the bitter rain.

Then the silence was broken by the soft chant of the women. The words spoke of unending sorrow, unending faith. Their voices at last trailed off and were lost in the sigh of the falling rain.

When the last woman had departed he heard a commotion at the edge of the village. Hunters had returned with game: four deer, several geese, and a string of rabbits. It was not a rich harvest; the deer were lean after a hard winter, but their arrival was welcome. The game was left near the lodge entrance and the six hunters entered to see the Chief. Alonqua entered just behind them, stood off to the side and listened. The Chief expressed gratitude for their efforts, their timeliness and their presence.

"We have little time," he told them. "The soldiers are less than two days distant . They travel as swiftly as White men do when they know what they want. I have spoken with the elders. It is agreed we will go when the sun sleeps and the moon rises. It is only a few days before the Full Frog Moon and we will have light to begin our journey."

In the hunters' eyes Alonqua saw bitterness and shame that they were too few to fight the soldiers. The eyes of the Chief revealed a man struggling to lead a retreat to a home they might never find. "We have only time to harvest the meat, to preserve a portion with our fires. The rest we will eat as we travel. Our caches of corn and beans are nearly gone, but we will have enough food to take us where we need to go."

Turning to the hunters he said, "Eat now and rest a little. You need to be strong for the journey."

To the elders he added, "Tell the people to gather what is precious and what is necessary for warmth. Tell them we will gather at the setting of the sun."

In a moment the lodge was empty save for Alonqua and the chief, who looked at him with steady eyes.

"I am grateful for your return from your journey so that you may join the people once again. You are young, but your eyes reveal what you have seen and what you have learned. In your heart I see the heart of Mawenteh, and we have need for the wisdom he has passed on to you."

Alonqua's responding words came hard, but he knew his path.

"My Chief, I am honored in your trust—but I will not go with you."

The words hung in the air. The sound of the rain on the lodge roof grew louder, as if the rain were striking all of the Earth.

"Why will you not go with us? Has your journey taken you to a place above your people? Can you no longer join your heart to those who love you?"

"While I live I have no choice but to breathe, and while I breathe I must be one with my people. I trust that soon I will join this journey. For now—I have my own. For now—I am called to remain here."

"I do not understand, Alonqua, you will be missed, but a calling must be honored. You know the path we will take. *Manito* grant that you will join us in our new home in the west.

"But you are weary. You must rest."

"I can help the People prepare for the journey."

"Until you rest, my son, you can help no one."

He offered the Chief his hand.

"I will do as you ask, my Chief. *Wanishi.*"

He left the lodge and entered a world he struggled to embrace. On the way to his hut he saw no one; all had retreated to their shelters, from which rose curls of smoke. Even now his people were drying strips of meat for the long journey.

Near his *wikewam* he found a sputtering fire tended by River-bird Woman. On her lap nestled a little girl. Alonqua knew her as Alana, who, like himself, was a fatherless child. He knelt beside them and held out his hands to the fitful flames. From the fire the old woman drew a burning stick. Alana looked up at Alonqua and graced him with a shy smile. Alonqua returned the smile and offered his warmed hand to her.

"River-bird Woman, how is it you tend this fire under weeping skies. Surely you and the child would be warmer and drier in the *wikewam*."

She looked up at him with eyes old as the Earth, deep as the night sky.

"Soon we will leave our home. Until then I choose to keep this fire alive. Remain with us if you will, just for a little time. Your presence eases my heart."

He placed his hand on River-bird Woman's shoulder and she reached up her free hand and placed it over his. Kneeling before the fire he awaited her words. She pointed to a stack of dry sticks sheltered under a mat of woven grass.

"Each stick is a memory. One by one, I place them in the fire, and in the flames, I see my life unfold."

She fell silent and reached down to touch the Earth.

"This place is my home. This sky is my roof. My mother and father settled here when I was no older than this little one. They, and five other families, had journeyed from the East. They had been driven out, their village burned, and they found this place and made it their home. You know all this, Alonqua, but the words are restless in my heart and I must share them."

She looked off into the forest as she stroked the hair of the little girl.

"I remember them telling me that this was a good place, rich in game and sweet water, and that it was far away from the Whites, and that we would be safe. For a time, we were."

She turned her eyes toward the river and the high ridge far beyond.

"I love this home. I love the river and the way it sings to me. I know every tree, every sacred stone. They are a part of me. And now my husband is dead, but I know his spirit lingers here. And when I leave here, my heart will be torn, like the roots of a tree that has fallen in the wind."

He could not tell whether tears or rain moved down the deep-furrowed cheeks. It might be he thought her old eyes had no more tears and that the sky was crying for her.

"I asked Alana's mother if I could bring her child with me to the fire. I want to share my memories with her. I wish her to hold this place within her heart and take it with her to whatever home awaits her."

The old woman looked up into Alonqua's eyes, into his heart.

"I would stay here, Alonqua, but I know the people wish me to join them. They mean well and I understand they fear for me. I will not go against their wishes. But only my body goes with them, and it will give way soon. These feet will not touch the Earth beneath the next home, if ever the people find one. My heart remains here."

Alonqua's words fell gently like the rain.

"For a time, Chosen Mother, my body and my heart will remain here as well, and *Manito* willing, I will join the others. While I am here, I will look for your heart in the river, the stones, and the trees. I honor you, River-bird Woman."

"*Wanishi,* Alonqua. I recall the little boy you were and I see the distance you have traveled. Mawenteh was just your age when our people settled here. He learned what was sacred and good in this valley, in the river and high on the ridgetops. In his eyes I saw the same gentleness and strength I see in yours. He gave to me a piece of his heart, Alonqua. I know he has given this heart-gift to you as well, my son, and that piece, joined to your own heart, has touched the stars. *Weli Kishku,* Chosen Son."

"*Weli Kishku*, River-bird Woman. I will look for you at the setting of the sun."

He turned once again to the low flames, then pointed to the sticks.

"May I have one of your memories to light my fire?"

"Yes. I have many sticks and can easily spare one for your

fire. Choose any you like."

He knelt and drew out one that was dry and pale, like an ancient bone. Holding the stick in the fire, he watched the tip bloom into red flame. River-bird Woman took Alonqua's hand and looked deep into the fire-flower.

"You chose well. It was a happy time—when I was a child and I learned the language of the birds."

She released his hand and once again stroked the hair of the little girl on her lap.

"And so now, Alana, let me tell you about the birds and how they spoke to me."

The soft voice of the old woman was soon lost in the sigh of the rain. Shielding the fragile flame with his cloak, he reached the hut and pulled open the door. The inside was a dark hollow place. Faint strips of daylight sifted through the bark walls.

He reached for dry kindling and wood sheltered near the fire pit, and then to a cache of fur blankets hidden beneath a mat of woven reeds. He gathered together a bed of wood chips topped with dry threads of elm bark. A few more chips above, a touch of the flame, and the fire-seed sprouted. Some twigs and the flames grew—a few larger pieces and the fire burned brightly, lighting the walls and warming his heart. For a time he sat by the fire. Perhaps he thought of the other fires around which families gathered. It might be he saw the little ones seeking comfort in the arms of their mothers and fathers.

Not long after the sound of rain faded and the wind freshened. He walked to the door, opened it and took in a long breath of spring air. The clouds were thinning, breaking up. The air was cool, but it carried the scent of new life. Closing the door he turned to the furs and spread a deerskin on the damp earth. Upon this he set another, and he lay next to the fire.

Like the talons of a young eagle releasing a branch for its first flight, his heart let go and he flew in the sunlit sky. And then the sun faded—and he slept.

Chapter 19
FAREWELL FOR A LONG TIME

Alonqua awakened to distant voices and the soft tread of many feet. The morning rain had given way to late afternoon sun, and he opened his eyes to cracks of golden light creasing the western wall. Then, piercing his heart like a cold spear point, the truth of this day.

"No—wait!" he cried out, throwing off the deerskin and scrambling to his feet. "Wait! Until I—"

"Bid them farewell?" The voice came from a dim shape lost in the shadows. "'*Lapich Knewell?* I will see you?' Or '*Owapicnoway?* Farewell for a long time?'"

"Temetet? You! Why are you here? Where are—?"

"The people? Do not fear, Alonqua. They would not leave while you are sleeping. They would not want that! Besides many feel we will have a change of heart and join them."

Temetet stood and handed him a bowl of steamed cornmeal and venison.

"Sit Alonqua, and eat. There is time to talk of what we will do before the people leave."

Alonqua searched the eyes of his friend and then sat, placing the bowl at his side.

"It is good to see you, Temetet. Can it be only two nights have passed since we talked in the Valley of Stones? Already it seems like long ago."

"Much has happened since that night Alonqua."

"Yes—and much is about to happen—but I ask you—Temetet, you speak of 'they' and 'we.' Why? Your eyes shine with an angry fire. You cannot think of staying here with me—of not…"

"Of not leaving with them—*our* people? And why is it I cannot stay? Strange, Alonqua, that it is you who tells me I cannot! You choose to stay and fight. Even the Chief does not say to you, 'Alonqua, you cannot.' No one has said that to you. Not to the great Alonqua! It is true you have changed—but not so much. Many think that you have found great medicine on your journey—that Mawenteh has gifted you with wisdom. Maybe this is true, but you are not so powerful—not so wise—that you can say *I cannot* do as I wish."

"Temetet—my friend—I am sorry. I spoke without thought. I have no right to say 'cannot' to anyone. But can it be that you chose—as I spoke—without thought?"

Temetet clenched his fist and struck the earth.

"I *have* thought! Why do you ask that? Does anyone question *your* thinking? Most believe you remain with your new medicine to fight the salt-eaters. They believe you remain to stall the soldiers so they cannot pursue our people. I will help you, Alonqua. We will not be driven away like *pukwes*, the mouse!"

Temetet raised his fist and struck the earth once more.

"We will fight them as brothers!"

Alonqua set the bowl aside, rose, walked to a corner of the *wikewam*, knelt, and retrieved a small flat stone. He then placed more wood on the fire and waited until the flames rose and the dark spaces brightened.

"Mawenteh wished me to keep this stone. He said that I would someday need it. He spoke true—now is that time—Temetet, hold the stone close to the fire and tell me what you see."

"I see a stone."

"Move it closer to the fire."

"There is nothing here to see—maybe a stain, a dark stain, right here at the center, but that is all."

"You are right, my friend, and that is all you need to see."

He reached for the stone and pointed to the little hollow in the stone.

"The drop of blood gathered here. It is dry now and faded, but two autumns ago, that blood was alive and it moved through the body of one who crossed a sacred line"

"What has this to do with me?"

The day was waning; soon the moon would rise. There was little time.

"Two autumns past I was fishing along the river. You might recall the water was low and on both sides one could walk with the river and work the deep holes where the fish gathered. Though the season was late, the air was warm. It was hard to think the cold of winter was just days away.

"As I fished the sun drew close to the western ridge and cast its light down and across the water. As far as I could see, both up and down the river, were clouds of golden fliers, little insects, a river of life drifting just above the water. It was strange to see them there, but then I saw something stranger still—a shape darting here and there—whirling—hovering—flying through the golden swarm.

"At first I thought it a bird gone mad, but it was no bird. It was the night-flier, *Pipisilunkon,* the one who hunts the insects in the darkness. We have all seen him pierce the lights of our fires on summer nights, but here was one in the light of day, feasting openly. My thought was that it had found a little den to sleep away the winter, but the warm days stirred it to one last hunt. I watched this strange dance until the sun touched the ridge and shadows began to rise from the river."

"Pipisilunkon moved like this—with little grace—up and down—darting this way and that, snatching up each flier. The bat was greedy, his only thought to feed and stuff his belly before the long sleep."

"Then, from the forest across the river burst a feathered spirit. *Nenhil*, the bird-hawk, had been watching just like me. Now was the time to strike. The falcon flew fast and straight, like an arrow of grey fire. *Nenhil* struck the bat in mid-turn, spinning him round and round. Then sharp talons plucked the bat from the air as fruit from a tree. The hawk bore his prey just above me, and I heard *Pipisilunkon* cry out like a wounded mouse. *Nenhil* drove her talons deeper. No more cries."

"The attack was so swift, so deadly! I was stunned. I sat, heart pounding, until I reached out my hand to rise. You hold the stone my hand touched. The blood and my finger met. The blood of *Pipisilunkon* fell upon the stone, and here it remains. If you stay, if you try to fight them, this blood is yours."

His friend reached out for the stone and touched the blood stain.

"I am not *Pipisilunkon*, and yet you say the blood is mine. How can that be?"

"*Pipisilunkon* has one great strength—the Creator places in him the gift of knowing the darkness. Under the cover of night he flies with grace and purpose. There is nothing to harm him but *Ghokos,* the owl, who would rather find his prey on solid ground. By day, the strength is gone. The animal that shed this blood crossed into a world of danger and he paid with his life. Pipi was awakened by a warm day and sought one more meal. You are awakened by invaders who take our home and you seek to fight them. The reasons are of no importance. Some lines must not be crossed."

Temetet placed the stone in Alonqua's hands.

"Temetet, the stone is yours. When you are angry and seek to fight those who drive us away, look at the blood and know you must do only that which is within your power. Like *Pipisilunkon*, the strength of our People is to fly through the night, to survive and hold on. Times will change when we may again challenge the hawk in the light of day. That time is not now. Keep this stone close. Someday pass it on to another who needs it more."

His friend rose and spoke.

"I hear your words, and I understand. But why, then, do you stay, if not to fight?"

"Temetet, I only know what I cannot do—I cannot leave with the People—and I cannot fight the soldiers. What I will do I do not yet know. I trust the answer will find my heart."

Alonqua opened the door and together they entered a world

of magic light. The sun's journey across the sky was over. The golden light poured softly down the western ridge and settled upon the little village by the river. The wind had turned, and flowed from the South. Like the very breath of spring it whispered up the valley, bringing with it a wordless prayer of new life.

The People had gathered at the heart of the village, awaiting the chief and the elders who were just emerging from the Council Lodge. In his hands the Chief cradled a clay urn. He stood before his People and placed the bowl in the hands of the nearest child.

"Hold this gift, Little One. Feel its warmth. It is right that you touch first, for it will be the children who must hold this piece of fire and carry it into the days and years to come."

The child held the urn and she looked around with eyes wide with wonder.

"The children know best," he said. "Like all of us they are troubled, but they know with their hearts what is true. They know we rest in the Creator's hands, as this piece of our council fire rests in the hands of this pure heart."

He paused and looked upon his People.

"This ember from our fire, held within its bed of ashes, will travel with us. We will feed it each night of our journey and carry the new fire-seed with us each day. When we find the home that awaits us we will dig a pit, surround it with stones, gather the wood. Our new fire will be born of our old fire. And so our story will not end here."

Silence settled on the village. The sun touched, then melted into the ridgetop. Twilight rose from the river and flowed across the village. The Chief looked to the warriors and spoke sternly.

"There are some here who would use the fire from the lodge to burn this village. They are angry, and I understand their anger. These homes we have built and tended with our hands. We have slept here, eaten here, celebrated here—mourned here. To some the thought of the Whites burning this village is unacceptable. Some would wish to stay and fight, but they know they must live to protect the families. Some of you have spoken that the eaters of salt find only ashes—that they be robbed of their pleasure."

The Chief met the eyes of each of his people, the children, the grown men and women, the old ones—and into the eyes of Alonqua.

"Know this! WE are the Village. These shelters, these fire pits, this Council Lodge are only the bones of one whose spirit is departing. Without the People, they mean nothing."

His voice hardened and his words recalled the sound of iron on stone.

"Let the Whites burn the bones. Let them laugh at what they do. Let them feel their power. And let the burden of what they do fall upon their own hearts. Alone, in the night, they will awaken and know the truth of their actions. They will know that they did not so much burn a village as dishonor the Creator. And for this they will feel shame. For this they will pay an untold price."

As the last light to the west faded, to the east a silver glow softened the darkness, Chief Nighthawk pointed to the urn, held in the hands of a child.

"This is the only fire that matters, the fire that will light the dark nights ahead. Carry this, Little One, and when you grow tired there will be another waiting to hold this fire."

He turned to his people and spoke with a voice that carried the tone and rhythms of ancient People, all those who had been forced to leave a home and find another.

"You have gathered what there is to gather. Each in your own way has bid this place farewell. The sun has set and the moon rises across the river. Now we must go—quickly and with no thought of what has been, only to what will be."

In silence, under the shelter of a soft spring night, the People stirred. The dogs were called. Burdens were lifted and placed on shoulders, and children were summoned. The moon, nearly full, had broken free of the forest and entered the sky. The long moon shadows pointed the way. Each found his place. Chief Nighthawk raised his hand and gestured to the west, and the living heart of the village bones moved as one, a solemn procession seeking a place—a Home.

One lingered; it was River-bird Woman, and she came to Alonqua as he stood before the Council Lodge.

She reached out and touched his heart as she had done so many times. Her free hand held a small deerskin packet bound with sinew.

"Alonqua, the People wait for me. I must be brief. In your *wikewam* you will find a gift. I have left it near the fire—it is my farewell to you—deeper and truer than any gift I can offer."

Her little hand spread wide as if to hold all of his heart.

"Accept my love, which I give to you now freely, as I have from the moment my husband guided you home."

River-bird Woman moved her hand from his heart to his cheek, touched his tears.

"My once little boy. You were hurt and lost. And we found you. Alonqua, I fear you are hurt again—but you are not lost. No matter how lost you might feel. Your heart knows the way. You are a boy no longer. Now is the time to receive this. Mawenteh carried this weight until his spirit passed. Now, for a time, it is yours."

Alonqua's hands received the packet,

"Chosen Mother, I am grateful for this gift, whatever it might be. But why did Mawenteh not offer it with his own hand when I left him on the night of rain?"

"Alonqua, I did not say what you hold is a gift. Far from it. What you call a 'gift' is far too heavy to carry through the hard journey to find your heart. No one, not even you, can carry what you hold and still fly to the stars. Now is the time. Mawenteh has always known this."

"But I am still lost, River-bird Woman. And now feel I am yet that little boy you once held as I cried in the night."

"No, Alonqua! I can no longer speak your spirit name, but we both know the truth. Anyone who has eyes and heart can see what strength rests in you. And you are not lost. You understand far more than you know. Trust!"

The old woman placed her weathered hands upon his.

"As for what you hold—what you call a 'gift'—I can say only this: within the deerskin rest four stones. One is a gorget stone. The others are spear points. Mawenteh found them long before you were born, locked in the roots of a fallen oak. He believed them to rise from long ago times, the time of ice and snow, when our tribe was young."

Mawenteh looked down at the deerskin surface, fingers tracing hidden shapes.

"The Old Ones," he whispered.

"Yes, Alonqua—The Old Ones."

"River-bird Woman. In the Valley of Stones—with Temetet! I heard them—I heard the drums—not like ours—deeper—slower, like distant thunder. The Old Ones! I felt their eyes upon us. I spoke of this to Temetet. My friend was not eager to stay."

"I am not surprised. What you heard and felt was not meant for Temetet. Nor were the stones meant for Mawenteh—except to find them and guard them. Many times he longed to hear the story of the stones you hold. Pieces of the story would rise only to melt away. He carried the stones deep in the forest, held them under the moon, and still the stones did not speak. But from the moment he held you in your darkest time and led you our home, he knew. He knew he was but keeper of the stones—the bridge to you. Alonqua, you are The One. And know this—Mawenteh does not choose you. The Old Ones choose you."

Alonqua shivered as if touched by fingers of ice.

"They choose me? Why? Choose me? For what?"

"My Chosen Son, the story of the stones is very old. It clings to life. The story of the stones—whatever it might be—this story is true, and it is right, and it must live on. The Old Ones lived the story and placed it in your hands. Alonqua, now you are a part of their story as The Old Ones become a part of yours. And now it is you who will live the story."

"And whatever is true and right will never die—Mawenteh's words!"

"Yes, Alonqua, Yes!" The old woman's eyes glistened in the moonlight. "Now you begin to see. This night, hold the stones. See them with your heart. Return to the Sacred Place where stone and water meet. There you will live the story—be one with it—and the story will rise from the sleeping stones like a warrior from his bed, to do battle on this Sacred Earth for what is true and right.

"Now I must leave. But it is here I leave my heart. Look for me in the gifts I love—the new leaves, the smell of spring, the songs of the river birds as they tend their young. *Owapicnoway*, Alonqua."

River-bird Woman once more reached across and touched his heart, then reached out her arms and drew him to her. A brief embrace, a kiss on his cheek and her voice—one last time—rose from her heart.

"Alonqua, this night, when your heart is low, you will find strength. Trust!"

Before he could respond, before he could find words, she turned and walked away. The People, aware of her absence, were waiting. But, as she rejoined them, they still did not move on. All eyes rested upon the dim figure standing in the heart of the Village.

From some distant hollow the call of *Ghokos*, the owl, spoke of the mysteries of the night. And in response to the call, Alonqua stepped forward. Perhaps he wished for the right words, the right way to wish them well—offer hope—bid farewell.

But his People were too far away, and he did not have it in his heart to draw close. The time for words had passed. Instead he stepped back and knelt. Never taking his eyes from his People, he reached down to touch the moist Earth. Then he stood and placed the same hand on his chest. Those closest saw his hand tapping out the rhythm of a heart, the heartbeat of the Earth, of his People, and of his own.

The child with the urn saw first. Perhaps she was one who watched him fly above the Valley of Stones. The little one smiled and knelt, touched the Earth, rose and touched her heart. The child next to her followed, and then his mother and father, then other families, then the elder men and the Clan Mothers, the warriors and the Chief. All tapped their heart in rhythm, as if the whole village were one shared drum.

Only when *Ghokos* called out once more did the People turn, hands still on hearts, and begin to move down the path. Alonqua watched them until the last of them disappeared into the silvery river mist.

And now he was again alone—holding the packet tightly

with both hands, Alonqua looked around to see the empty *wikewam*—cold—like blocks of ice under the moonlight. Before turning to his own dwelling, he lifted his eyes to the moonlit sky searching for his friend, the little star. At last he found him, but there are times silence is best. And so as he gazed up, the star gazed down. Somewhere in between they met, and that was enough.

Once inside he placed the packet on a stone near the glowing coals. Nearby lay the gift, a silvered twig nestled on a bed of cedar fronds. There would be time to see what lay within the soft deer hide, but just now a memory sought release.

Alonqua knelt close to the shimmering coals and touched the tip of the twig to its center and closed his eyes.The newborn flame burned pure and white as the snows of winter. The fire followed the path down the stick like a setting sun. Just before it touched his thumb, the white flame flared once and was gone. Alonqua looked at his empty hand with eyes of wonder.

"I cannot repay this gift, Chosen Mother—nor would you wish me to. I know you receive my gratitude as you walk upon the long path. I close my eyes again and again I see you turn, reach out to me—and smile. Your memory! Haha! You are a little girl. It is morning. You sit on the bank and you smile as you watch the sunrise paint the ripples on the river. Eagle appears—from nowhere—vast dark wings trailing ribbons of mist. White head shining like sun on snow—night-black talons clutching a young pike! Haha! I see you nearly fall in the river. But I see her yellow eyes turn to you. She sees you! She cries out—you reach out to her with a smile to match the sunrise!

Alonqua opened his eyes, rose and looked out into the night.

"Your smile! I will remember! The moment lives—your memory of *Opalanie*—of you—when she cried out and your eyes met—this moment will not be lost. I will tell my children—and they theirs. It will not fade. *Wanishi,* River-bird Woman. *Owapicnoway.* I will look for you in all that true and right—in all that lives on and never fades."

Turning from the night, Alonqua softly closed the narrow door and looked upon the bed of glowing embers. The little packet, resting on the stone called to him. Slowly, very slowly, he knelt and reached his hand to touch it. Then lifting it from the stone, he closed his eyes as if to see beneath the soft deerskin.

"Four stones," he whispered. "So heavy for something so small."

Part Three

Chapter 20
THE STORY OF THE STONES

The *wikewam* was warm, but the dying embers held little light. Still holding the packet, Alonqua used his free hand to gather dry cedar sticks. Kneeling before the gently pulsing coals, he held on tight to both as he searched for words to release a troubled heart. One hand opened slowly, and one by one the sticks fell upon the packed earth floor. The other hand held the deerskin packet above the coals. He fixed his eyes upon the sinew binding, and he struggled to still the tremor he heard in his voice.

"What have you left me, Mawenteh? River-bird Woman tells me what I hold is heavy. It is *very* heavy, Mawenteh! She says I have been chosen! I ask again—where *are* you?"

Alonqua listened to the silence—peered into the darkness all around. No voice—no vision rose to comfort and guide him through the storm raging in his heart. Instead his own empty hand found the way.

One by one, as they were released, the sticks returned to his hand. In seasons to come he would speak of this moment as if from a waking dream. Had the sticks risen to join his hand? Or had his hand, with a mind of its own, found them in the darkness? What power moved him to close his eyes, break some sticks and leave others whole, and to set each stick in its place upon the dying coals? When at last his hands were empty, they joined and settled in his lap. He opened his eyes and drew in a long breath. His hand moved to his shoulder, disappeared beneath his tunic and touched the scar.

The cedar smoke rose in the stillness of the hut, passing through the roof opening on its journey to the stars. Alonqua drew close to the smoldering sticks and blew softly. The Fire-eagle sprang to life—fiery wings soaring upon an ember sky.

"Mawenteh! You do not speak! You will not appear—so is it your hand that guided mine to shape my spirit name in words of fire? If you are here—if you have moved my hand to restore my courage, *wanishi*! But this is not enough!"

Alonqua watched as the flames melted into the glowing coals. He shook his head and stared into the darkness.

"Can you not see, Mawenteh? My courage is the flame! One moment here—the next gone! I cannot feel my spirit. I am a stranger to my name! I am a stranger to my People who do not know me! They have moved on. And now I fear you do not know me. Mawenteh, I do not know myself! I am not Sapelei Opalanie. I am only a boy who sleeps in a shelter that will soon be in flames. I am alone! I have never been so alone—more alone than the night you found me."

He looked down to the packet resting at his side.

"And now you have left me this."

Reaching down, Alonqua closed his fingers around the hide-bound stones and lifted it to his eyes. He breathed deep—once—twice—again. Placing his hand on his heart, he smiled a faint smile, a cold dawn upon a dark face, a cold dawn far better than none.

"What have you left for me, old friend? Whatever I hold might not be so heavy under the stars."

Once outside the *wikewam* and under the moon, Alonqua gathered more wood and lit the fire. When the flames leaped and danced, he knelt, holding the packet with both hands. The sinew cord wound round the deerskin, bound with a knot so tight, so strong, none but he could solve it. The knot was Mawenteh's secret—a secret he revealed to Alonqua late on a long winter's night. Mawenteh described it as a binding to hold and protect what is precious, until the sacred moment of release. If the bonds were cut, the magic would perish unborn. As Alonqua's fingers unraveled the mystery; it might be he thought of *Kwenoomuk* and her children. But this knot needed no blood to loosen it, and soon the packet lay in his hand—contents still hidden—but now unbound.

Breathless, corner by corner, Alonqua lifted the soft deerskin away from the objects which lay within its folds.

Revealed in the firelight were three flint spear points resting upon a small, smooth flat stone. One point was white like the snows of winter, one rose-red like the dawn sky, and one black as the darkest night. He held each of them in turn close to the fire, observed the sleek, dangerous shape, like a large willow leaf, and the delicate deadly workmanship evident in the blade edge. The arrow and spear points of his people, even the steel points, appeared primitive in comparison.

Alonqua turned his face to the Great Marsh, and his voice trembled as he spoke.

"Mawenteh, what prey were they meant to bring down?"

He placed the spear points at his side and gazed upon a flat stone roughly the size of his hand. A hole had been drilled through at either end, suggesting this was a gorget stone, intended to be worn at the neck. Alonqua held the face of the stone to the firelight. At first there was nothing to see. Then, as the flame grew brighter, shapes emerged from what appeared only to be formless scratches. These shapes coalesced into a desperate battle.

Roughly drawn human figures brandished spears as they challenged a strange beast compared to which the men seemed as children. Spear shafts protrude from the eye and belly. One of the "children" lay beneath the foot of the beast.

"Mawenteh, I begin to see the story of the stones! I remember the stories you told of the Old Ones. You spoke to me of their world—of the ice and cold. You spoke of the broad river, the sacred places—and that the Old Ones are our ancestors—and that the Lenape have come Home."

Alonqua traced his fingers around the outline of the great beast.

"And you spoke of the animals the old ones sought, of their

size and power."

He reached for the spear points and held them next to the etched stone.

"And the weapons they crafted to bring them down."

His eyes were drawn to the hunters—to the one lying at the foot of the beast.

"These are not children. These are men, brave men. And some of them die to feed their families, and the beast dies to save his herd."

Alonqua closed his eyes. Still holding the stones, he turned away from the firelight and raised his eyes to the Heavens. From the sky, from the Earth, from the Great Marsh rose the faint deep pulse of ancient drums. He drew in slow breaths: one...two...three, and opened his eyes. The Moon, afloat upon *Opitemaken*, the River of Stars, cast her gentle light upon him as he held the stones—alone in the heart of an empty Village

Alonqua shook his head and rose to his feet,

"*Piskeweni Kishux*, you are good company. But you do not speak. I look to my friend, the little star. I cannot find him. I am sorry, Mawenteh. You do what you can. You all speak to me, all reach to me. But now I do not know how to listen. And I am alone. And I do not know how to be close to anyone."

Holding the stone and spear points close to his heart, he retrieved a burning stick from the fire and carried it into the wigwam. There was more cedar near the fire pit, and soon Alonqua lay next to a new fire, one that offered just enough light to look once again at the stone.

Though he was very tired, the stone perhaps opened to him as though an archway to another world. He sat up and stared at the stone, at once wide awake. Alonqua's breath froze in his throat, even as the stone grew warm—warmer than his hands, and then the whispered question "Whose hand held this stone—while the other hand told the story?"

Once again, his fingers moved across the surface, tracing each line over and over until at last his fingers grew still—and he closed his eyes. And then—his finger moved once more—slowly…slowly…up…then a little to the side…up again…and there it came to rest. Alonqua moved the stone close to the fire, and lifted his finger.

There, near the edge of the slate tablet, etched with the faintest of lines, a seated figure looks upon the hunt. No eyes nor face reveal expression, but the figure leans towards the hunters. The head tilts to the one who has fallen.

"Who are you?" he breathed to the lone figure scratched in stone."

The call of *Ghokos* broke the spell. The drumming ceased. Alonqua placed the gorget stone and the spear points upon the deerskin. With the sinew cord he bound the stones once more with Mawenteh's knot. One by one, the singers of spring raised their voices to the stars—and to Alonqua.

As he lay upon the furs, he placed his hand on his heart. Doubtless on his mind were many questions still to be answered. But he must have let them go—for he smiled, a real smile.

Perhaps he was not alone.

The last flame sank into the glowing embers. For a moment the sound of distant drums rose in the night. Alonqua placed the stone and the spear points beneath the furs and strained to hear more. But soon the drums faded and the songs of the *sikon taleka* joined the darkness.

Before the singers of spring lulled him to sleep, he prayed for the departed ones—his people—moving to the West, away from present danger but toward an uncertain world. None save the very young, carried by their mothers, would sleep this night, nor the next.

Somewhere in the moonlit forest *Ghokos*, the owl, called out to him, joining her voice to the chants of the little frogs. Alonqua closed his eyes and listened to those singers of spring whose voices rose and fell with the breath of the night.

And then there was a time when all was silence—and he slept.

Chapter 21
THE DARK WOLF

"The soldiers! They come this day—to burn the village."

His eyes opened in fear and dread. Gray dawn light was sifting through cracks in the bark walls. The fire was long since dead. The little spring callers who had sung Alonqua to sleep, were silent.

"Do not fear Little Ones," whispered Alonqua as he sat up and reached out for a pouch of dried corn and venison. "Do not allow my fears to silence you. No soldiers come to burn your village. Spring will come. No soldier can stop its coming. Sing this day, even as the smokes rises—sing of spring."

Rising and moving past the entrance, Alonqua made his way to a nearby spring pool. There he sat, and gathered his heart for a hard day. One by one, the little frogs called again, until the water's edge rang with their songs. A cool breeze touched his face as he watched columns of mist rise from the water. By now the birds had joined the frogs and Alonqua listened to them call back and forth. Some, like *Mukwinunt*, the blood-colored bird, were winter survivors, rejoicing in the warming land. Others, weary after a long journey from the south, spoke softly of their travels.

Soft spring grass bordered the pool—glowing green even before the first days of spring. Patches of watercress had risen above the shallows. He pulled a small bunch of stems and leaves from the pool, sat on a log, and opened his food pouch. Alonqua chewed slowly, thankfully. Despite what lay ahead this day, he savored the crunch of parched corn, the toughness of the small chunks of meat, the tenderness of the greens. They tasted of the only place he had ever known.

Perhaps Alonqua thought of the many sacred places scattered across the valley, and that he would wish to visit them before he would leave—never to return. Many he knew from Mawenteh—burial sites, places of power. Many he had found himself on solitary journeys to find peace. Perhaps he wished to hide them, protect them from what was to come.

But there was little time. Only two sacred places mattered. One, where water and stone met, he would visit this night, beneath the Full Frog Moon. The other was on a flat shelf of land perched halfway up the ridge above the village. This place had been Alonqua's choice because he knew his mother loved to come there when she was troubled and needed to be alone. And now, when he reached her grave, there was no memory stone, no mound—only an oak sapling. Alonqua had planted the acorn there, just next to where he and Mawenteh had placed her body. It was how she had wished it.

And now her son, Alonqua, sat against the great mother oak from whom he gathered the seed. His face was to the rising sun. It would be hard to know what thoughts and visions rose up in his mind, but he was soon distracted by a small gathering of *Chihopekel*is just above him. Their wings were pieces of the blue sky darting from branch to branch, their songs brief and gentle questions back and forth. Then as one of the bluebirds flew to a nearby tree, a single feather caught on a twig, teetered in the morning breeze, broke free and drifted toward him. When it came to rest alongside he picked it up and smiled at the bird.

"This is good of you, my friend. *Wanishi.*"

Alonqua rose and walked to the sapling that, a moment ago, held the wing feather. Standing there for a moment, he raised the gift to the light.

"This is for you, my mother. As the bird gave to me, I offer her gift to you. Within my pouch rests the twin—the blue feather you gave to me when I was a little boy. May this feather bring peace to you—and my love—as your gift has brought me many times on lonely nights."

With his knife he cut a shallow slit in the narrow trunk and fixed the quill end firmly in place. Alonqua knelt, steadying his trembling hand on the narrow trunk of the little oak. There was no time to linger—and no need.

"*Owapicnoway,* my Mother," he whispered as he rose. "Your love is with me ever, as I trust mine is with you. I am well. Be at peace."

Between the grave of his mother and the Valley of Stones the ridge makes a broad turn, draws close to the river, and curves away again. It was here he froze at the distant sound of metal on metal.

Nothing he had learned, neither in refuge in the lodge of *Temakwe*, nor on his flight to the stars, had prepared him for this. The soldiers had come at last. He had hoped not to be there; he had hoped to be gone. But he was there, high on the ridge above the empty village, and he could not hide his eyes from what was to unfold.

Many men were moving swiftly on the River Path. Voices drifted up the ridge—excited, confident voices. He crawled closer so that he could see the village and already there were several men, advanced scouts, scouring the *wikewam* for any stragglers.

Time froze. The Earth held its breath. The sounds of the advancing soldiers ceased and all was still. The land lay before him. His eyes traced the horizon and settled in the heart of the valley, even now filling with golden morning light. The distant trees glistened with the faint green haze of swelling buds. Beneath the trees were the places he knew well. To the South was his Mother's resting place, to the West the open deer meadows, to the North was the Valley of Stones, to the East, first the empty village, then the river, then the Great Marsh.

The village had been the heart of his home, the river and marsh its lifeblood. The trees and animals not only shared his home, they were a part of its living spirit, a part of his own spirit. It was this home, this valley, that had borne him, cradled him, challenged him. He knew each old tree, each deer meadow, each deep hole in the river. The village was dead, and the heart was gone, but perhaps he remembered the one most sacred place—more enduring than the village, more ancient than even the world of the Old Ones in the Valley of Stones.

Alonqua looked out across the valley, east across the marsh, and rested his eyes upon the place where sacred water touched sacred stone. In the moment of stillness spirits of the forest gathered around him. They shimmered in the shadows and shadowed the columns of light.

"What do you want of me?" he whispered to the spirits. "I can do nothing—nothing."

The first gunshot was followed quickly by another, followed then by distant shouts and laughter. One of the dogs had remained in the village hoping for a handout. Instead it had received a ball of lead and was even now pawing the earth in its death agonies.

From his place above the village, Alonqua saw the dog's pain and he heard the laughter as more blue and green-coated soldiers swarmed into the village. He watched each dwelling entered, searched, abandoned, torched. Several soldiers entered the Council Lodge, and Alonqua felt a moment's gratitude that the soul of the village fire was already far to the West, safe from those who would extinguish it forever.

Alonqua sensed the disappointment of the soldiers that the village was empty. There was no one to kill, no food stores to be destroyed, no loot to be pillaged. Alonqua turned his eyes once more to the dog, now still, then to the flames licking at the walls of the council lodge, then from *wikewam* to *wikewam*, as one by one each felt the torch. Then he lifted his eyes from the village and onto the river, and from the river to the ridge, and from the ridge to the heavens, and even there his eyes found no peace, for the smoke from the many fires had already risen and stained the sky.

But it was the laughter that tipped him over into the place of darkness. It was the laughter of those who had no love for the Earth—who would bend the Earth to suit their needs, who held nothing but contempt for those who called this place Home. It was the laughter of the conquerors, of those who knew they had the power to impose their will in any way they chose.

The laughter entered his heart like an instant poison, and his sorrow blackened into hate, and his grief into rage.

He called out to the trees, to the deer, to the fish in the river, the birds of the sky.

"So it is this you ask of me—to fight for you. You cannot speak to them. You cannot tell them to respect this place and who know it as Home. You have no words to tell them what they should know. And should you find the words and the means to speak, they would not listen. They feel their power, and they laugh at their shameful victory."

Before him rose a hickory sapling, dead for want of sunlight. Teeth clenched, his hands clutched the narrow trunk and wrenched the tree from the soft earth. He broke off the few branches, then the top. The root ball, dirt-covered, was as hard as his heart.

"Temetet was right! There are times, Mawenteh, when the dark wolf must be fed. I'm sorry, my friend, but I cannot stand and watch this."

He held his weapon with both hands struck the earth—once.

"I will fight for you!"

Twice.

"I will die for you—but, *Manito*, grant me a little time. Fill them with wonder at my presence—that I, just a boy, dare defy them. Just a little time—time to crush a skull—and before they raise their guns, grant me another—and if the first ball of lead misses my chest—one more! And then—their lead will be their gift to me!"

His journey began with the slow walk of a war chief on his way to his last battle. But as he drew closer, the laughter stirred his heart into rage. And so his pace quickened, step by step. At last, rushing headlong, nearly to the village, sucking in a quick deep breath to shout his defiance, a blow to his chest, hard and sure, dropped him. He clawed at the earth, desperate for his stolen breath. At once he felt his body squeezed, pinned down by an irresistible force. Struggling to free himself—to live—to breathe,

Alonqua managed to turn his body. Between his eyes and blinding sun through swaying branches, a shadow in the shape of a man spoke his name.

"Joshua!" Alonqua gasped.

A sudden blow to his jaw stunned him, and while his senses returned, Joshua spoke in a low whisper.

"Be silent—be still. You are not meant to die here. You say I saved your life there in the marsh. Why do you think I saved you? Not for this!"

Joshua reached out his hand, grasped the crude club from Alonqua's grip and flung it away. All fight drained away from him; Alonqua found his breath and awoke as if from a dark dream.

"And so, Joshua—you save me once again."

"Can I let you go now? For your size you fight well, and I'm tired."

"And for one with so kind a heart, you strike hard."

Alonqua, who had come so close to dying, intended his words to lighten his heart, but when he saw the shadow cross Joshua's eyes he wished them back.

Releasing his hold on Alonqua, Joshua crawled behind a fallen log and motioned for Alonqua to join him. The soldiers, so occupied with their search of the village, did not notice the thwarted attack, nor the timely rescue. Even now, their shouts and laughter broke the stillness of the morning. Joshua saw the rage rise once more in Alonqua's burning eyes.

"No, Alonqua, it's over. We cannot fight this fight."

Just as the word "we" settled into Alonqua's heart, the wind rose. The sky spoke of danger as dark clouds raced beneath the sun. The heavy air rushed past them and toward the village where it funneled its power into a raging whirlwind. The soldiers looked fearfully to the sky as the wind drove flames across the village. They screamed in pain as fire and sparks touched bare skin and ignited clothing. The soldiers, so arrogant upon their entrance, fled the village, themselves set ablaze with their own fire. Most sought the river for deliverance, and from the river, one by one, they slowly emerged, dripping, nursing wounds.

As fast as it had come, the wind died down, and the sunlight found creases in the thinning clouds. Articles of charred clothing—tunics, trousers, caps—littered the smoldering village. One of the soldiers reached down to retrieve his gun, then pulled back his hand in pain. It was too hot to touch.

The arrival of several men on horses, uniforms bright and crisp, awakened the dazed and fearful men. Sharp voices, stinging slaps from the flat side of sabers organized the men into loose columns. Their remaining uniforms were singed and full of holes. As the village emptied, as the conquering heroes departed, no one spoke.

No one laughed.

Only when the last of the ragged column had disappeared up the trail did Joshua reveal his bewilderment.

"The wind...out of nowhere...the burning soldiers..."

Alonqua looked long upon the smoking remains of what had once been the heart of his Home, then turned to the man at his side.

"The wind did not come from nowhere, Joshua. You know our language, and you tried to save us from harm. I think you must know of *Mesingw*."

"I have heard the name spoken, but I know little, only that *Mesingw* is a Guardian Spirit, but that is all."

"Yes, Guardian Spirit of the trees and animals—of the forest and river. Only days ago it was *Mesingw* who guided me to save a mother otter just before you saved my life. Perhaps it is *Mesingw* who brings you here to save me a second time. The wind you felt was *Mesingw's* anger. It was He who fought the battle we could not fight. It was *Mesingw* who turned the flames onto those who brought them."

Alonqua's jaw hardened.

"But *Mesingw* cannot stop what is coming. He can only remind the takers, as he did today, that there will be a price to pay for the harm they do."

Joshua chose not to speak. His eyes searched the forest as if for some lingering trace of the Guardian. At last he took a deep breath and pointed up toward the ridgetop. "I have a camp there.

Not much. But there is food, a fire, and moss for a bed. I'd be obliged if you would join me."

"*Wanishi*, Joshua. Before dark I must join my path. Until then I am grateful to receive your food and your company."

Just before he turned to follow his friend up the steep slope he looked across the marsh to the Sacred Place at its heart.

"I am coming," he whispered.

Chapter 22

BRIDGE OF ASHES

Joshua's camp rested in a place Alonqua knew well. Perched atop the ridge in an opening of the forest, the setting spoke of many wanderers who had come to find peace here. Time had exposed the stone of the ridgetop and in the creases and hollows soft moss gathered sunlight and invited rest.

Reaching the camp, Alonqua smiled and spoke.

"You have chosen a good place to rest. Mawenteh, my Old Friend, gifted this place with a name. He called it *Aspitunk Pilsu.*"

Joshua reached into a heavy cloth bag and drew out two rabbits. As he knelt to skin them Alonqua continued.

"These are old words, not often used. *Aspitunk* means 'high place,' not just a high place like the top of a ridge like this, or the top of a mountain or a tree. The word means more closely 'a place near the heavens, close to the stars.' Our tribal name is *Lenape.* You might know it means 'common person.' *Pilsu* means a person as well—a human, man or woman. But not just anyone. *Pilsu* is a man or woman whose dark spirit has been granted light."

Joshua did not look up nor pause in his deft skinning and butchering. Only when he had taken skin and guts to a nearby rock as a gift for the ravens, only after he rinsed the blood from his hands and dried them on the moss, did he speak.

"Your friend was wrong. That name is a lie."

Joshua speared the skinned rabbit with a sharpened stick.

"This is yours. I think the fire is hot enough now."

Alonqua received the gift and held it over the low flames. For a time the two sat in silence as the sun drew near the land across the river. Only when Joshua's eyes rose to meet his steady gaze, did Alonqua find his words.

"My brother—Joshua—there is nothing you can reveal to me that will change my heart to you. You have given me my life—twice—but if you think that these are the gifts that bind my heart to yours, you are wrong. I know you. I know who you are and what you are. You..."

"You know nothing of me—nothing of my heart. What I know is that the name your friend chose for this place is now a lie. As long as I remain here, it is a lie!"

Joshua reached for the second rabbit, speared it, and placed it near the flames.

As the meat began to sizzle and sear, silence rose once more. Somewhere high above they heard the rasping cry of a soaring hawk seeking his home. The fire had ebbed to hot embers, and upon these Alonqua placed the sputtering meat.

"I will not ask again, Joshua. I have no right to ask anything of you. Only your trust—I will say this and no more. Mawenteh did not lie—does not lie. Nor is he mistaken. The truth of this sacred place drew you here. This place does not judge you."

They ate in silence, and when the meal was finished, Alonqua, mindful of his promise, did not speak. Instead he rose to fetch fresh wood for the dying coals. Joshua reached into his pouch and found his pipe and tobacco. Alonqua watched his hand tremble as he held a burning stick to the tobacco. Joshua's eyes darkened. And still Alonqua waited.

The sun had slipped away. Dusk settled upon the ridge, while far below the river animals welcomed coming night. Joshua tapped his pipe on a stone near the fire, took in a deep breath—his eyes searched the darkening sky. Finding no refuge there, he looked deep into the fire—and spoke—his voice the merest whisper.

"He looked like you, Alonqua."

"What did you say? I could not hear."

"I said he looked like you! Do I need to shout?! Not as tall, but your age, your eyes. When I saw your eyes that day near the Beaver Lodge, I thought you were the same boy, and that he had come back to life."

He set the pipe on the stone and looked away from the fire and down the valley.

"The boy had done nothing wrong. It was not that he was or ever would be a threat to us."

Joshua's voice grew calm and even, as if what he would say had been rehearsed a long time.

"The boy was at the wrong place at the wrong time, that's all. At the time I was a scout for the same soldiers you saw today, and I was good at it. I did my job and was paid well. I helped the soldiers know of the movements of the tribes, especially of the Shawnee and Tecumseh, who, until a few years ago, was threatening to retake the Ohio Lands. I learned from your Chief that your Father died fighting with Tecumseh. I said I envied him. The chief did not understand. Maybe you will."

Joshua's voice trailed off and he took in another long breath to steady himself.

"I have seen some bad things, Alonqua, I have lived them. In the years I was a scout—I had been a target many times—wounded twice, once with a musket ball, once with an arrow. Those wounds healed."

An orange-red glow, like a fading fire, lingered in the western sky. To the east, above the distant hills soft silver light foretold of the rising of the Full Frog Moon. Joshua reached for a stick, broke it, and tossed the pieces into the flames.

"There had been a killing. A white settler and his wife shot and scalped—his boy child taken—the cabin burned. The settler had been warned he should leave, that the piece of land he chose was in an area no longer secure, and that he was in great danger. He was stubborn and spoke that it was his land, and he wasn't about to give it up. Some would say he had asked for this. But, Alonqua, when I saw the bodies something snapped in me. I had seen bodies, many bodies. Some were soldiers, some settlers like these. I had seen the bodies of your people. A few I killed with my own hands. All of that I managed somehow to shut out. Not this time."

Until this moment Joshua's gaze had been locked on the fire. Now Alonqua felt those dark eyes searching his own, eyes so dark that Alonqua willed himself not to look away.

"I won't make any excuses for what happened next. I could tell you I was tired, hadn't slept in three nights. I could tell you I was angry and fed-up. I could tell you the way the woman looked lying face-up, eyes open, tore away something inside. I could tell you I got caught up with the other scouts and a squad of soldiers who came upon the bodies, all tired and bitter like me, swearing vengeance. None of that matters. Nothing excuses what I did that day. And what I didn't do."

Joshua removed his hat and ran his fingers across his forehead then through his hair.

"I was a good scout, but not good enough that day. We lost the trail when it crossed this very river where it joins the Muskingum some miles to the South. By all accounts they were not members of any one tribe, just a band of roaming Indians, dangerous, angry, and lost, just like us. Anyway, losing the trail was a bitter pill. We sought blood for blood, and one way or another we would have it."

His voice softened and Alonqua leaned close to hear the words.

"He was just a boy, Alonqua, just a little younger than you. He had been out hunting I imagine, had strayed too far after a wounded deer, something like that. No one cared why he was there, but it was on this boy that all of our anger spilled. But from the moment we bound him I knew in some deep way that this was wrong, and that I wanted no part of it. I think the boy knew that and he looked at me until the moment a final knife thrust ended his pain."

His own pain spilled over in a rush of words.

"Don't you see? When I saw the boy—really saw him—I knew this was wrong. I did not strike him or hurt him. But I was silent. I did not protest. I did not stop it. To have killed him with my own hands would be better. Maybe then I could forgive myself. But to have known it was wrong—to have the chance to stop it. I did nothing! Alonqua, I see his eyes each time I close mine. It was his eyes I saw when I looked at yours that day near the marsh. Don't you see? Can't you see?"

Again Joshua turned away, his body trembling like a reed in the wind. Alonqua used the silent time to choose his words.

"I see, but through my eyes—not yours. Your guilt blinds you to the truth of that boy. Just before he was killed—when he looked to you—what did his eyes tell you?"

"I saw his plea for my help. That I should save him."

"I did not ask what you felt in your own heart, or what you wished you would have done. What did you see in his eyes?"

"I told you. He wanted…"

"No! Joshua, I know that boy as I know you. He knew you could not save him. You would have been killed had you tried. The boy knew that! Those men wanted that life and they were going to take it. Somehow—because your heart tends another way—your feelings changed. You knew this was wrong—you feel you should have stopped it even if you died trying. That is how I felt when I ran toward the village to kill as many soldiers as I could—I wished to die fighting. You saved me to do what is true and right. Joshua, I tell you I know that boy, and I know that from the moment he was captured he knew he would die."

"Are you saying that when he looked to me he wasn't…"

"Asking you to save him? No! Let that thought go! Drive it out! What he was asking of you was not to save him. His eyes asked you to *remember* him—and this you have done. And in honoring his memory you have saved twice the boy who sits before you. In the days to come you may save others."

Joshua reached for his pipe and placed it in his pouch.

"It will take time," spoke the tall man, "but I hear your words. Someday I might even come to believe them. But Alonqua, this is not yet done. I have more to say."

Joshua stood and met Alonqua's eyes with the light of hope.

"When you leave here to join your People, I ask to join you. The ways of my people are no longer my ways. The day after the death of the boy I left the soldiers, wandered the land and lived apart. I no longer feel any part of that world. Over the past winter I have come to know your People, I have traveled with them, hunted with them, learned your language. Your ways lie close to my heart."

Again, a moment of silence, broken at last by the words of one brother to another, not of the blood, deeper. The words were hard, but there was no other way.

"Joshua, we Lenape believe that each should follow the path of his Spirit. No man should stand in the way of that path. If to join with us is truly your path, I cannot stop you. My people will not stop you. But I will ask you to think hard. It might be your true path is not that of my people."

"Alonqua, I have thought hard, so many times I can think of nothing else. I am a good hunter. I love the land and have studied the ways of your people. I can help you weather the storms ahead. I can..."

"Joshua, this is hard to say—I know you mean well, but you can do nothing for us. My people do not desire your help—we have no need of your pain. We will have enough to do to stay alive, to hold on to our stories and our ways. The one way you can help us—or yourself—is to find your path among your people. Not the path you walked before. A new path."

Alonqua reached out and scooped up a handful of ashes and moved his hand to a space between two stones.

"My brother, do you think that I can take these ashes and form a bridge from stone to stone? A bridge strong enough to hold even an ant who wishes to cross?"

"No, Alonqua, a bridge of ashes cannot join. It will hold nothing."

"And your path to my people will hold nothing—least of all you. That path will be a bridge of ashes."

Releasing the ashes, Alonqua waited for the words, just as Mawenteh had done so many times when he spoke to a boy who had lost so much.

"I know your sorrow. I have lived it. I know what it is to feel I am alone—a stranger to those around me. Nothing would please me more than to see you as one of us—to see you live whole and free, far away from all that troubles you now. But that cannot be. Should you come with me, your troubles will follow. Your People will follow and soon the new village will be ashes as is this one. And then on and on until there is no place left to go."

Joshua rose and walked a few steps to a large stone the size of a small *wikewam.* He placed his forearm against the rough surface and rested his head on his arm. Alonqua turned in the direction of the marsh and felt the time drawing near when he must leave. Still, he waited until Joshua turned from the stone, strode across the silent moss and stood before him.

"I will not go with you, Alonqua, but the thought saddens me. The path back to my people will be hard, and there is much in that world that sickens me."

"My friend, it is only through the actions of one like you that the sickness can be cured."

Alonqua listened to the night air as if to hear the faraway tread of feet moving west. Far below, nestled near the river, a ghost village slept. Alonqua leaned close and spoke.

"These are dark times for my people—each day finds fewer of us and there are too many of you to fight. Joshua, our ways are fading—dying—but the Truth at the heart of my people must go on. My friend once told me all live in one Village—all the People—red and white. We share the Village with all that is alive—the animals, trees—the sky, the water, even the old stones beneath us. He said to me that your people want no part of this Village. He feels his power. He rips apart the Village of Life. He wounds the Earth to meet his wants. But Mawenteh believed and now I believe a time will come when the people of your world will feel lonely and empty with their greed and power. The wounded Earth will return to you hurt for hurt. Your people will be afraid. Many will wish to rejoin the Village of Life. They will wish to join the Earth and Sky rather than rule them. But they will not know how. The times of my people are dark, but yours will be darker still. Without good voices among you—true hearts—to light the path back Home, your People will be lost. And they will know they are lost."

Alonqua cast his eyes toward the rising moon. Picking up a stick he stirred the ashes releasing a shower buried sparks.

"Do you see, Joshua? Hidden beneath the ashes? The seeds of a new fire. Mawenteh is here—now—he speaks now with my voice. And we say to you that you will return to your people. You will stir their hearts as I stir these ashes. And your children will stir them. And their children. And one day from the many sparks fires will be born—and the fires will join—and the light from this Fire will be the Truth that brings you—all of us—Home."

The two sat in silence. Alonqua closed his eyes and mouthed a silent prayer. Then, as if moved by one heart, both rose. Beneath the River of Stars, even now fading with the rising moon, two hands clasped and held on.

"Joshua, *Nihmat*—Brother!"

"Alonqua, *Nihmates*—My brother!" returned Joshua.

"May *Manito* be with you."

"And with you," spoke the man who had saved his life.

Alonqua released Joshua's hand and turned away. As he worked his way down the moonlit ridge, he looked back only once, back up to *Aspitunk Pilsu*—to the high place of the Pure Spirit.

And he smiled to see the flickering glow of a new fire.

Chapter 23

SACRED SILENCE

The night child of the setting sun and rising moon awakened and opened her eyes. So, too, did the *pemakamiksit*, the creatures that roam the darkness. Alonqua heard them all about him, their soft touch upon the Earth, their whispers to their little ones following close. He looked up through trees as if to hear the slow breath of the living stars.

There was a time he might have spoken to them, perhaps to the little star now rising above the forest, or to *Xalaputis* weaving her silvered web high in the branches, perhaps to *Pukwes*, the mouse, stirring the leaves beneath his feet. For he was now alone in a way he had never known. But as he traveled the river path one last time, he must have also known that for now the time for words had passed.

Pausing in a forest clearing he felt for his medicine pouch, then the white feather resting on his scarred shoulder. His other hand squeezed the soft deerskin holding the spear points and the etched stone. They were with him—and so he moved on.

Between the High Place of the Pure Spirit and the canoe that would take him to the Cradle of Stone lay the charred bones of his village. When he reached this place he moved to skirt around it as one would a body whose soul has departed. But pausing once more he looked upon the place of his youth. Whatever his thoughts, whatever feelings rose in his heart, cannot be known. He did not shed tears, for some things lie deeper than that, but when at last his feet moved he found himself approaching the heart of what was once his home.

As he neared the torched *wekiwam* of Mawenteh and Riverbird Woman he looked up to see a door that was no longer there. He entered a dark lost space and gazed upon walls that had melted into ashes that very day.

Alonqua knelt before the dead fire and reached out for a handful of soft ashes. The other hand crushed a fragment of charred bark that had fallen from the roof. His cupped hands formed the vessel which held his past. Alonqua pressed the ashes, gray and black, to his face, then into his hair, then down his neck and over his heart. If there was a prayer, it was silent one. If there were tears, they were lost in the darkness. He bowed his head, rose and walked away.

Mawenteh's old canoe, tethered to a driven stake, greeted him at the riverbank. As Alonqua ran his hand along the damp smooth side it is likely he recalled Mawenteh telling him how, as a young man freshly arrived in the valley, he burned and carved the canoe from the trunk of *muxulhemenshi*, the tulip poplar. "This tree is the best," he once said to Alonqua. "The wood is soft for carving, But it is stronger than willow, lighter than elm. And so you see, this canoe is still here. It is still strong. It carries me easily from place to place, which," he said with a chuckle, "is more than I can say for these old bones."

And now the old man who had said these words no longer held his own carved paddle that guided the canoe for its final journey. Alonqua's hands held the well-worn paddle, his grip firm and sure. Seeking the swiftest current, he turned the canoe downstream toward the hidden channel.

And so his journey found Alonqua where he had begun it. This time there was no hiss of rain on the water. Now upon his final journey into the Great Marsh, the night air did not hold the chill of that earlier time. Alonqua had traveled very far in many ways, since the moon was young. It is likely he was very tired, but his paddle stroke was strong, deep and true. The stars offered little light, but he knew the way well now, and soon he turned the canoe deftly into the hidden channel. Emerging into the Great

Marsh he did not pause to stand atop *Temakwe*'s lodge to find his water path, nor was there need for the guiding cries of *Kwuskwutis*. Alonqua paddled swiftly, weaving among islands of reed and buttonbush. All the while he scanned the brightening sky above the eastern ridge.

The nearby splash of a night-roaming fish startled him. Were it another time but this, he might have spoken to *Names*, bid him good hunting. Not now. Instead, Alonqua pulled the paddle from the water. He turned his eyes to the North. Somewhere in the darkness lay the Island of Light, serenely awaiting the Sun of the Night. Soon the little pool nestled atop the Tree of Life would receive her light, and the frog and the spider, and all the living things hidden there would stir and look up.

Alonqua turned his eyes again to the East, where, above the ridge a softly glowing sky foretold the rising of the moon of *Xanhanni*, the Full Frog Moon, the Moon of New Life.

Between Alonqua and the Tree of Life lay *Aptachute*h, the Place of the Frozen Heart, brooding in silence. There the light would be sucked away. Alonqua's jaws clenched and his eyes grew cold. He moved his hand to the white feather, and he raised his eyes to look beyond *Aptachuteh* to the wounded tree that had healed. And when he turned to rejoin his water path he looked again to the ridgetop where the distant trees caught and held the rising moon as a silver net holds a silver fish. And then she broke free, free of the net, into an ocean of sky. The moon released her light in a gentle rush, and as it flowed across the Great Marsh, Alonqua smiled. Once again the paddle rose and fell, rose and fell, leaving a trail of silver swirls.

It might be that the heart hears the distant sigh of falling water long before the ears; no doubt it was so with Alonqua, who often spoke to Mawenteh of hearing *Sukpehelak* whisper in his dreams. Though the Sacred Place still lay in deep moon shadow, his heart listened and his canoe stayed true to his path. And when the whisper at last rose from his heart to his ears, Alonqua again smiled. He spoke no words of greeting. There was no need. *Sukpehelak* knew him well—knew he had kept his promise. He had returned.

Alonqua nestled the canoe in a little cove near the Great Stone. He felt for the medicine pouch, and beneath the fur cape, near his heart, the packet. Strong hands found a firm hold on the stone, and he pulled himself up and onto the crown of *Ahsen.*

With great care he placed the packet and pouch upon a little bed of moss growing near the edge of the glistening pool. He removed his fur cape and leggings, then his breechcloth and beaded apron. As he looked upon the doeskin apron, adorned with eagle and lightning, he moved his hand to his scarred shoulder, then approached the dark, trembling pool.

Alonqua knelt in the heart of the Cradle of Stone, and *Sukpehalak* received him as a mother would a child. He did not shiver nor cry out, though the water still held the chill of winter stone. Instead, he trusted to *Sansun Mimens* to hold him safe, as upon his head, down his shoulders, chest and arms, fell the tears of *Supkehelak*—until they touched his heart.

As the ashes washed from his body, Alonqua closed his eyes and turned his face upward. It may be that, one by one, the hurts of his life rose from a deep still pool and joined the rivulets of gray and black coursing down his body. Perhaps the form of his Father rose before him, appearing as the strong warrior striding off to join Tecumseh. And when he reached out his hands he might have touched the hand of his dying Mother, and the hand of his departing friend before he sent Alonqua on his journey. And when his tears joined the cleansing flow, and the last ashes flowed from his skin into the Cradle of Stone it may be that the burning village once more rose before him. If so, this hurt, too, was washed away.

Then there was only the light, not of leaping flames, but of the stars—and one thing more.

For now the Full Frog Moon, the moon of *Xanhanni*, had broken free of the high ridge. The shadow had passed away and the stone and water glistened in the sacred light. High above, in honor of her coming, nearby stars faded and were lost in a silver sea. Alonqua, breathless, shivering, stepped out of the pool and stood erect, arms held out—*pampiwesu*—naked as the moon and stars. Had Alonqua opened his eyes he might have seen a skein of night-flying *menkixu*, swans of the North, moving fast to the land of *Ahsen's* birth.

It might have been the chill of the Spring night that at last opened his eyes. We come from the stars, but while we walk the earth their fire cannot warm us. And so after donning breechcloth, leggings, and fur cape, he knelt once more, spreading the beaded doeskin apron upon the face of *Ahsen.* The Full Frog Moon hung like a silver lamp from the roof of the sky. Beneath this healing light Alonqua reached for his pouch, loosened the drawstring, and as he did in the Valley of Stones, placed each gift upon the stone.

First was the sky-blue feather of *Chihopelekis,* the gift of his mother. The blackened bark from *Xaxakwe* the Healing Tree, found its place, followed by the ear stone of the great fish. Alonqua placed at his side the clam shell gifted by *Kwenoomuk,* and then set the tuft of sweetgrass gathered in *Temakwe's* lodge beneath the blue feather. Within the little nest of soft marsh grass he uncovered the shell fragment and acorn. Together they found their place amid the gathering.

The snow-white feather called to him, and he turned his eyes to see it resting upon his shoulder. The gift of *Opalanie* had not failed him—not on his journey to the stars, nor his easing the pain of a troubled brother, nor all the trials between. Alonqua unwound the red cord from the feather, then from his hair. With the cord he formed a circle around the gifts, then placed the white feather at the center.

The deerskin packet still lay upon the patch of soft moss, a little green island upon a sea of silver stone. Alonqua drew very close. Beneath the moon tiny droplets of waterfall spray were glittering stars adorning a lush forest. Reaching for the packet his hand hesitated and withdrew. Again he reached out, touched the deerskin. Again his hands pulled away, as if the etched stone and spear points had at last found their home and wished to stay. A third time he reached out, this time only to unbind the knot—and slowly, gently, corner by corner, he revealed the contents to the waiting moon.

He slid the soft skin from beneath the stone. The black spear point he placed to one side, the white point on the other. The third, the color of a sunrise cloud, he rested just above the etched stone.

Alonqua sat back and looked upon what he had placed first upon stone—a piece of bark, two feathers—one sky-blue, the other snow-white, a tuft of grass, the ear stone of a great fish, the shell of *Ehes* the clam, a fragment of an egg, and an acorn —all encircled by the red cord.

He looked next to the little bed of moss, to the spear points and etched stone at rest at its heart. He had nothing more to offer. And what more could be done?

Already the Full Frog Moon's journey across the sky was halfway over. Whatever was to happen, whatever he must do, must happen—be made to happen—soon.

Closing his eyes, Alonqua breathed deeply—and waited.

And then, from somewhere across the Great Marsh, beyond the river, beyond the ghost village, perhaps from a hidden valley strewn with ancient stone, rose the sound of drums—faint but strong, faraway yet so close as to mesh with the beating of Alonqua's heart.

He opened his eyes and reached out, and the gift of *Kwenoomuk* received his hand. Within this shell, he placed another, the fragment from the shattered nest. He reached out his other hand to touch the swirling water. A few drops were enough. With the aid of the ear stone, he ground the eggshell and water to a fine white paste. His finger, moving from shell to face, placed four marks tracing a path from cheekbone to nose. Four marks—four winds, four seasons, four stages of life, four stars, rivers offering blessed water to the Earth. Mawenteh spoke often of the truth of this sacred number.

Alonqua had remembered. And now as his eyes rested upon the Full Frog Moon, the ancient drums rose and fell with the breath of this sacred night. And the Moon, gazing down upon his upturned face, beheld eyes of quiet faith and wordless wonder.

"It is time," Alonqua whispered.

CHAPTER 24

HANDS ACROSS TIME

He took a deep breath, gathered himself, closed his eyes, and waited.

For what he did not know.

Yet from all around him, above—below, something was stirring, awakening, as if a Spirit, very old, very powerful, that had been asleep for countless winters, was opening its eyes and preparing to rise.

Alonqua no doubt sensed this awakening. Searching the night in all directions, he rose slowly, urging his voice to address this mounting presence.

"What is happening?" he whispered. "Not a breath of wind—nor the splash of a fish—not a ripple. The moon on the water is the twin of the moon above. I look up to see *Xalaputis*—so still—not weaving—her web half-made. The forest lies silent. The animals—I feel their eyes—they watch me. They wait."

Summoning courage, Alonqua spoke again, not as a whispering child, but as one reverent and unafraid.

"Who are you? You are not Mawenteh—not his spirit. My heart tells me you are ancient as the drums I have heard in the night. You are not *Mesingw*. I saw *Mesingw*—I followed him—I know that power—felt it. *Mesingw* moves. He sought me—found me. You do not move. You have waited here—and now I have found you. I ask again. *Who—are—you*?"

The stillness became a living thing, yet not alive, like an egg about to hatch. Alonqua, hearing no answer, drew close to the falling water. He knelt, lifted the white feather of *Opalanie* from the stone, and looked upon it: the strong shaft, the soft filaments. Beneath his breath the feather quivered as if alive. He placed the Eagle's gift upon his scarred shoulder and held it there. And then he closed his eyes.

It might be that behind his eyes he flew in the storm. Or that he recalled, upon his return from the storm, the eyes of River-bird Woman as she cradled his head in her hands. Or that he saw again the brave mother carry across the marsh a piece of a shattered nest to begin again.

None will ever know which came to him first. Was it the thought of the voice, or the voice itself? In truth, it does not matter. Perhaps once in a lifetime, perhaps twice, these two are one.

Seek...him...

Alonqua opened his eyes and turned them slowly to the falling water. Drawing closer, he held his breath.

Seek...him...A-lon-qua.

He placed the feather upon his heart, tears filled his eyes, shining in the moonlight, then spilling over, flowing down like *Sukpehelak's* sacred water.

"Mawenteh!" he breathed. "Mawenteh!"

Alonqua turned his eyes from the flowing water and looked upon the rippling surface of *Sansun Mimens*, as if searching for a face.

"Mawenteh! Your words, 'if the heart is clear, voices of our ancestors rise from falling water.' I understand now why we came here that day late in summer—when you asked for my silence so that my hands might explore the stone—that my ears listen to the falling water."

Yes-s-s...

Alonqua reached out to touch the moon's reflection.

"And why I felt my hand tremble as if the stone were alive! I asked you why—I remember now! You said to me, 'I, too, feel great power in the Stone. But not as you do, in your hands. *Ahsen* chooses not to speak to me, through hands or ears. Perhaps someday, he will choose to speak with you.'"

Yes-s-s...

Cupping his hand, Alonqua drew water from the pool to his burning forehead.

"And Mawenteh! You spoke of *Manito*—that when *Ahsen* was born—when the Earth was young—*Manito* thrust his hand deep into the fiery Earth and found him—lifted him up to feel the sun. Into all stones *Manito* placed power. Into *Ahsen* he placed a piece of his heart."

Yes-s-s...

Alonqua placed his hand upon the face of *Ahsen* and held it there.

"I feel it, Mawenteh—just as before. No! Stronger! The stone warms beneath my hand. Something old and alive is here. I have felt this ever since..."

Touching each of the four white marks on his face, Alonqua's mouth parted and his words were touched with wonder. "Ever since I laid out the gifts and placed these marks upon my face—Mawenteh, you sent me here to relight your fire and release your spirit. I chose to watch my people leave so I might return here—on this night—the night of the moon of *Xanhanni*—To hear your voice once more would be reason enough to do these things. But I know you, my friend. I know there is more."

My...voice...Ahsen's...words...seek the place...beneath the stone...

"Beneath *Ahsen*? How can..."

No...Alonqua...beneath...the stone...

Only one stone, the etched stone, lay within his sight, and he reached out to it—but once more pulled his hand away.

"Mawenteh, beneath the stone is moss, nothing more."

Beneath...

Gently, with trembling fingers, Alonqua lifted the stone tablet from the silver-green island and placed it in his lap. Then, so slowly, trying hard to keep the piece whole, he peeled the moss away. He leaned close, closer—his eyes grew wide.

Moist, with the traces of Earth that had gathered there over countless years, lay before him the clear imprint of a hand.

Drawn like a bird to its nest, *menanchi,* the hand of the heart, rose, hovered, and came to rest.

Two hands—across time—met—and meshed, fingers to fingers, thumb to thumb, palm to palm, in seamless union.

Alonqua had no time to smile a wondrous smile, to express his wonder to Mawenteh, to think a thought or say a word. Instead, he clenched his teeth, stifled his scream with an anguished hiss. His free hand reached across to his scarred shoulder, and he held it there, and as the moon of *Xanhanni* poured down her light, so tears of pain flowed from Alonqua's eyes, down his face and to the cold stone.

"Mawenteh!" he cried out. "Speak to *Ahsen*! Of the hurt! My shoulder! My heart! Is this—ah—a-a-h! How *Ahsen* speaks?"

Peace A-lon-qua...the hurt...will pass-s-s...

Had Alonqua wished to tear his hand from the stone—had he tried—the hand remained locked in its stone harbor.

"Mawenteh—my shoulder—the scar! I had thought it healed. It burns! A-h-h-h!"

A-lon-qua — your true name — Who-are-you?

"I am Sa-a-h-h-h! I am Sapelei Opalanie!"

Yes-s-s...look to...the feather...

The snow white gift of the Eagle lay on his lap beneath the stone tablet. Alonqua's free hand found the feather and brought it home to his burning shoulder.

As *Kwenoomuk's* pain uncoiled within the harbor of Alonqua's song, so the searing hurt from his scarred shoulder ebbed, breath by breath, as waves do once the storm has passed.

Alonqua looked to the hand still pressed in the stone print.

"Mawenteh—the pain—is gone. So much hurt! On my scar—but inside, too—my heart. That pain was worse! I have never known such hurt. No that is not true—once—just once—when—when..."

Your...mother...left you...

"Yes—when her spirit passed. That is how it felt, though I know it was not her choice to leave. But why do I feel this now? Why my scar? I only placed my hand here—on the stone."

The wound...of one...can heal...the wound...of another...if the two hearts...are one...

"What do you mean, Mawenteh, 'the wound of another.' What other? Tell me!"

And for a time there was only the music of falling water. Alonqua waited, tried to move closer to *Sukpehelak,* but his hand was the anchor that held him fast.

"Who is the other? Tell me! Mawenteh! Mawenteh!"

*Peace...A-lon-qua...this is...your path...I can do...no more...*Owa...picnoway*...I will...see you...on the River...of Stars...*

Ripping his hand from the stone, Alonqua scrambled toward *Sukpehelak*, nearly falling once more into the moonlit pool. The stone tablet and the forgotten feather lay in his wake, side-by-side, upon the stone hand print.

Alonqua searched the falling water, breathed in the cool spray, listening for the voice of a spirit who was no longer there.

"Mawenteh, you have left me—a second time. And Joshua—just now it would be good to share a fire. And my people each moment pull farther away from me."

His eyes grew wide, the faintest of smiles graced his lips.

"Mawenteh's words—'the wound,'" he whispered, "'of another.' Another. *Wanishi,* Mawenteh. I am not alone. The Other—is here."

His eyes fell upon the trinity: the tablet—the feather—the stone imprint, and he sat cross-legged before them. The stone tablet settled in his lap like an egg in a nest.

"It is time we meet. At last."

Chapter 25
UNTIL NOW

Then there was only the handprint in the stone. Once more his hand moved, only to hesitate.

"Not yet—not before I know I will not be hurt again—not now—not like that."

Moonlight filled the space. The impression glowed, beckoned.

"When I returned here I felt the heart of the Great Stone, *Ahsen.* Through the spirit of my friend, *Ahsen,* spoke. He spoke of—another—of you. The hurt was your hurt. I felt it. The hurt was—is—ours. And now, as I rest my hand—here—now—I ask again—*who are you*?"

And as his hand met stone, Alonqua was answered, not with a voice, not with pain, but with a sound rising from the earth like stone thunder.

The beating of drums! On this night and as before, the first night of his journey, again in the Valley of Stones. As then, these drums were not those of his people. And just now the beat was more felt than heard. The drum strikes, at first slow and heavy, the two-beat rhythm of a vast heart, grew ever louder, stronger, faster, rising from the earth to join the sky. The air grew colder; the wind rose and the forest moaned beneath a cloudless sky.

And then, as if challenging the drums, a cry pierced the valley like a driven spear. Alonqua had heard the sound once before late at night—alone—in the Valley of Stones. Then the cry had been distant, of another world. This was close, a long, high blast, defiant and vastly powerful, a Thunder-Being, not of the Sky, but of the Earth.

Alonqua stood, eyes ablaze with the battle-rhythm of the pounding drums, hands clenched as if holding a deadly lance. The drums ceased. The moon floated serenely, as before, in a cloudless sky and upon the unruffled water. His hands relaxed their grip, and he held them up to his eyes, as if surprised to see that they belonged to him.

He lowered his eyes from his hands to the stone, to the place another hand formed long ago, and to the stone tablet resting alongside.

The time to close the Great Circle had arrived. Alonqua quickly knelt and once more joined his hand to the hand he had sought since birth. His other hand lifted the stone tablet to the Moon of *Xanhanni.*

"I feel your heart. But I wish to know it. May this stone be the bridge where we will meet."

Alonqua lowered the stone tablet and held it steady. As a thirsty man drinks from the welcome spring, the stone received the moonlight. Beneath his eyes, hard stone dissolved and edges melted away. The etchings, each line, each detail, traced in silver light, took on depth, motion. Moon became sun. Dark sky became dazzling blue. What was once the Great Marsh was now as a broad river, its countless channels flowing between narrow gravel islands like wind-blown braids. Flecks of dust glistened in the sunlight, and the wind grew wild, carrying the scent of wet stone. Upon the distant riverbank rose a narrow band of green rushes and dwarf willows, and beyond these a sparse forest of pine and hemlock.

The great beast etched in the stone's heart emerged as a raging force, long thick fur rippling in fury, head shaking in defiance.

Near the beast three stick figures stood now as men—flesh and blood—brave hunters—brandishing long spears tipped with deadly points. Another lay at the feet of the beast. The mammoth lumbered into a shallow channel, lowered his head, lifted a tree-trunk foreleg and plunged toward the fallen hunter. Evading the death blow in a shower of spray, still holding a tipless shaft, he gestured to the others to stand away.

Tearing his eyes from the battle, Alonqua looked at the hand on the stone. Around the wrist was a deerskin band emblazoned with a jagged bolt of yellow lightning. He looked upon the other hand, trembling, gripping a crystal stylus upon a stone tablet.

Alonqua's eyes, if his eyes they were, returned to the man in the river, his face a mask of blood. He stood in knee-deep water, thigh laid open spilling blood, supported by one good leg and the shaft of a lance half again as tall as he. His white-streaked hair was long, bound by a red cord. His bare chest bore the dark scars of many battles. In swift motion he fixed one last spear point into the notch of the shaft. Again he motioned the other hunters to withdraw.

The mammoth towered above him, turning first one eye, then the other upon the lone man. Long plaits of gray wool hung from the sides and chest. His massive tusks, curled nearly double, were yellowed and cracked with age. Doubtless, thick fur hid the scars of many wounds. Two were fresh, one between eye and mouth, another behind the shoulder. Spear points embedded deep in the flesh urged the fast flow of blood, matting the fur with streams of bright crimson. Lifting his great snout to the sky, he called to his herd, his tribe, to stay at the river's edge safe from harm.

And in the end there was no final battle, just a brief dance of death. Each old warrior, each with grievous wounds, granted the other a brief truce. The herd-leader lowered his ancient tusks to the rushing water, then raised them to the sky, calling once more—not to the herd, but to one no longer a foe. The call, deeper in tone, rose above the river, echoed down the valley, not with anger nor with defiance, but with respect. Lowering his spear the dying hunter bowed to his foe, tapping twice flint point upon ivory tusk. Eyes met. Both understood.

The hunter planted his sound leg and thrust the keen point into the killing place between, then beyond the heaving ribs. And as the point pierced the great heart, the beast, with a mighty sweep of its tusks, found his mark, crushing the hunter's chest with a single blow. Together they fell. Together they released their spirits to the shining skies.

A boy seated upon a great stone bowed his head. Soft hand pressed hard upon the stone, so hard the hand whitened to the color of bone; so hard the stone gave way and received the hand—and the pain.

And then the word, in a voice soft as moonlight, lonely as a star.

"N'nuk."

Again. *"N'nuk!"*

Alonqua raised his head slowly. The sun, the river, men and beast were gone. The moon of *Xanhanni* ruled the sky, and the Great Marsh received her silver light. The stone tablet rested beside him. Once more, the markings on the stone lay frozen and silent.

He lifted his hand from the stone and looked upon it.

It was his hand.

Alonqua rose to his knees.

"And yet," he whispered, "this was no dream. I saw what I saw. I felt—still feel—what I felt."

He turned his eyes to the place where two hands met

"And you—you—are still here."

Alonqua gently placed the patch of moss upon its home, then rose to his feet.

"I heard your voice. I will always remember the sound of it. I will remember the word you spoke, *'N'nuk'* It is strange. Your word is our word. What my friend Mawenteh said to me is true. The Lenape lived here in your world of ice. Your world was ours. We are of the same blood. We hunted great beasts as did you. You were too young—were denied a place in the hunt. Upon this stone tablet you told the story—all but the end. You watched an old hunter offer his life so that a hungry village would have meat after a long winter. As he fell, you cried out *'N-nuk!'*—my father. Of course, *k'kuk*—your father. You watched him die out there on the river. The stone received your hand and your pain."

Alonqua reached out for the gift of his father. Rising, he held out the red cord.

"This cord I use to bind my hair. I saw such a cord—also red—upon your father. Did the other hunters bring you the red cord of your father, as the Shawnee brave brought me this cord from the body of my slain father?"

Alonqua nodded toward the spear points.

"And these—the great beast suffered three wounds—three spear points. Did they cut them from the beast, hold them in the river to wash off the blood, and present them to you? Did they speak strong words of the sacrifice of your Father—that the starving tribe had meat? I heard words, too—about my Father's courage in fighting the Whites, and that I should feel pride. Did I feel pride? No! I had lost the man who had given me my name. I had lost the father I never came to know. Did you feel pride? I do not think so. The pain I felt when I found your hand did not feel like pride."

The night was old; the day, child of the setting moon and rising sun, waited at the eastern gate. Alonqua opened the pouch and found the bluebird feather.

"I felt hurt when news came of my Father. That hurt was nothing to what I felt of yours. This feather is a gift of my Mother. Her death—I was there. I held her hand, but I could not hold her life. I felt her spirit pass away through my hands. That pain—that was like yours. And I wonder—was your Mother taken from you as well? Were you motherless—and then fatherless—a Child of the Tribe?"

"Did an old kind man find you—ease your hurt—offer you a home?"

Alonqua looked upon the patch of moss with eyes of sorrow.

"No, my Brother, I do not think so. I placed my hand upon Mawenteh's heart. He received my hurt. I fear there was no one for you—so you placed your hand here, upon *Ahsen's* heart. And he held your wound and the hurt for untold winters."

And then Alonqua turned to the Moon of *Xanhanni*, and the sorrow melted from his eyes.

"Until now."

As a child who has yet to walk, Alonqua approached *Sansun*

Mimens on hands and knees. Reaching the pool he gripped the edge with both hands and leaned out over the water. As he looked upon the rippling surface, along the marsh birds awakened and called softly to each other. The darkness above the towering ridge softened with the promise of a new day. And still he lingered, searching the heart of the Cradle of Stone.

And then there came a quick breath. And his sudden smile spoke of wonder. Alonqua reached out a steady hand and placed it flat upon the water. His mouth formed one word, scarcely a whisper, *"Wanishi."*

Just what, or who, his eyes found, his hand touched, there in the heart of the Cradle of Stone cannot be known, for he did not speak of it. Not then. Not ever.

Chapter 26
ENDINGS AND BEGINNINGS

One by one Alonqua retrieved the gifts of his journey and placed them in his pouch. The feather from the shining head of *Opalanie* came last. For a moment he hesitated as he held it alongside the red cord. But, slowly shaking his head, he placed this last gift gently upon the others.

Wrapping the deerskin around the etched stone and spear points, he swiftly made his way down to the foot of *Ahsen.* A few paces brought him to the remains of a fallen oak.

"So Mawenteh—my friend—here you found the gifts I now hold in my hand. And so it is to this place they must return."

Near the upturned roots Alonqua dug out a shallow harbor. Here the acorn, a sleeping spirit dreaming of Earth, found her home.

"Grow strong, *Kikishemanshi,* my-soon-to-be-born friend. In the seasons to come grow tall. Feel the winds, the rain, the blessed sunlight. I leave you as a gift to the Sacred Place so that you might someday receive a gift—a gift of undying truth."

Before covering the seed of the oak, Alonqua placed the snow-white spear point at one edge of the shallow pit. Upon the white he saw a spot of red, his own blood. He smiled, knowing well the points had lost none of their edge.

"You will guard the Eastern Gate which opens to the path of the Rising Sun."

He set the black spear point below and to the side of the first.

"You guard the Northern Gate—from which came *Ahsen,* the Great Beast, and the Old Ones."

Opposite the Guardian of the North he placed the rose point.

"You are the sentinel of the Southern Gate from which now, at winter's end, the warm winds will rise."

Alonqua turned his eyes to the West, out across the marsh, where the Moon of *Xanhanni* and her twin upon the water, held vigil on this sacred night.

The gorget stone rested in his hand, heavy with age. It might be that he felt the hand that held it so long ago.

"No, I cannot take you with me. You know this better than I. You would be a stranger to the place I must go. Brought here by a boy who is now my Brother, this is your Home. I place you at the Western Gate—at the doorway to the living past."

Alonqua lowered the stone and placed it next to the acorn, covered these and the spear points with fresh earth, and patted down the soil with a firm hand. Over this he scattered several armfuls of damp leaves.

Rising, he placed his hand upon his medicine pouch, loosened the string, and lifted the feather to the dawn. As he blew softly upon it, the feather quivered as though alive and ready to launch itself into a new day.

"I would journey further with you, but I am called to place you here, not far from the Giver—the Mother who had the courage to rise from the storm and begin again. Do you see that tree? Right there on the bank, bending over the water? It is *Telalakwe,* the sacred cedar. I will leave you here, joined to the tree spirit with the red cord of my father. His body found rest far away, and so now I invite his warrior spirit to come home—may the Warrior Spirit and the Mother Spirit join to watch over this sacred place."

Alonqua bound feather to cord, cord to tree. A dawn wind touched the feather, and it rose and fell as if to bid farewell. He then turned to Ahsen.

"*Owapicnowy, Ahsen,* and *Supkehelak*, may your spirits always meet here, in *Sansun Mimens*. There, in this Cradle of Stone, lives the Great Mystery—that what is true and right will never die. May the sun and moon shine on you. May you remain pure and whole. May you offer comfort to all the lost and troubled souls who come here."

Alonqua looked west to the Full Frog Moon slowly fading in the soft light of dawn. He withdrew his hand from the cold silent stone—both hand and stone now at peace. *Sukpehelak* whispered to Alonqua of her oneness with her ancient partner.

The hand that led Alonqua here had released him. He turned his eyes to the forest. Her paths, those of deer and men, called to him. He was free now to join his people. But he held back—one last time—just one more breath.

And then he turned and held out his hand as if to touch the living air.

"I know you are here—I know you linger before your journey , just as I. You will return to the River of Stars. With a heart free of pain. I will return—to my people still here on Earth. They are hurt. They search for a home where they can rest and heal. I want to help them."

His voice trailed off, then rose in shy laughter.

"My name is Alonqua! On the night I was born, my father held me beneath the River of Stars! They say my crying stopped and my eyes opened wide. My father named me after the stars! Does your name speak of the stars as does mine? Or did your Father find your name along the river, beneath a tree, beside a fire—or watching an eagle soar? I would wish to know your name—will you tell me in a dream? So I will know how to call to you when I am lonely—to call to you when—I..."

Alonqua shook his head and smiled.

"Forgive me. We are not little boys. Nor can we return to that world. And yet there is so much I do not know—and I feel I am very young—just now beginning. Do you understand? I regret I spoke like a boy meeting a new friend. I was only hiding from my sorrow. We have only just met—and now must part. And this saddens me, but—at this moment, upon sacred Earth, our hearts are one. We are not friends! *Nimate!* We are Brothers!"

Alonqua paused, waiting for his heart to speak once more. But first appeared the wonder in his eyes, and then the tears, and, last of all, his smile, rising like the sun.

"Until now, my brother—until now—I truly did not understand what my heart knew all along—what Mawenteh wished me to learn. No man, no woman, is ever truly alone. *Lapich Knewell,* my brother. We will meet again. Until then a part of you remains within me, as I trust some part of me will join you on your journey to the stars."

Alonqua withdrew his hand from one unseen—except by the heart. He looked once more upon *Ahsen,* upon the Great Marsh, upon the Earth where an acorn dreamed of sun and rain. He lifted his eyes to find hopeful *Xalalaputis* at rest in the heart of her silken web, then higher, to the crown of the morning sky—and beyond.

He drew in a deep breath, placed one hand upon his heart, the other upon a scar, and released the word.

"Wanishi!"

And as Alonqua entered the vast forest, his smile—and his tears—spoke of one whose heart was true. He knew his path. Whether traveling, as now, through a forest pierced with shafts of light, or upon a river cloaked in darkness and rain—he would find his way.

EPILOGUE

Some stories end. Many are lost—some just fade—and die.

Others, a few, go on and on. Just when such a story is about to die, it lives again, like the flame released from a fading ember placed upon a bed of dry bark. Both story and ember require a human heart to tend and nurture them—and the deep need to honor and preserve what is true and right for those who follow.

This is one such story, a new fire born of a single ember from a dying fire.

The story, from beginning to end, is a good one, but too long to tell now.

Another time…

But here is the heart of it.

~~~

A boy sits upon a huge stone. It is nearly dawn. Behind the boy, a trickle of water falls from a crease in the stoneface of a cliff. Beside him is a hollow in the stone; it is the size of a large kettle. The hollow is dry, awaiting the water that struggles to reach it, but no longer can.

Across the broad valley the full moon lies low, illuminating what was once a thriving marsh. Only a little water remains at its heart. The rest is cracked mud and withered reeds. The boy sees this. He sees bulldozers and excavators in rows beneath him, awaiting the men who will spark them to life.

This is now—a time of machinery—a time of progress. People live fast and so must move fast. City streets slow them down. A highway around the city is proposed so the people can
~~~

move faster. Marshland is cheap, and so the land and water is purchased from one who has neither walked nor floated upon it. He holds something called a deed. In this world that is all that matters. And soon much of the marsh is drained away—prepared for the morning the machines begin to topple trees and move the earth.

This is that morning.

The boy sits and waits. His heart overflows with dread. This boy is a little different. Amid the city, among people hustling through a world he cannot understand, he feels alone. The marsh, the stone and the waterfall have heard this boy's heart when no one else would listen. Here, in the rush of wind through the trees, the songs of birds, the voice of falling water, he has learned truths never taught in school. Only here can he feel he truly belongs. Only here can he feel he is truly not alone.

But just now he feels very alone, for in the distance a car door slams, then another, then several more.

He looks up to see the men in the dim light, strolling, chatting, entering machines designed to carry out the job the men were paid to do.

The first machine sputters to life, the boy closes his eyes and strikes the stone.

He calls for them to stop, but they do not hear his voice above the noise, nor would they listen if they did. As if to find refuge from an endless storm, the boy crawls to the hollow of the great stone and huddles there like a month-old bird in a nest, afraid to leave, afraid to stay.

The machines draw closer. A tree cracks and falls with a sickening "whump!"

"Not the old oak! He is my friend!" he cries as he rises to see the great tree still standing. Far too big for a bulldozer, two men with chainsaws approach. Eyes on fire, the boy shakes his fist at the machines. And his other hand he places on the stone…

"No. Damn you! NO! Not this tree! NO! No! No..."

He looks down at his hand at rest within the shallow print of another hand and his eyes grow wide.

And then—at that moment—the cry! A strange call like the

whinny of a sky horse, proud and defiant. He sees her flying fast from the west, snow-white head lit by the rising sun. Clutched in her talons is a stick, a foundation stick, charred and battered, but strong. Just before she reaches the old oak, she pulls up, wings fluttering. And there, at a joining of high strong branches, she finds the place.

A nest is born.

And that is very important because of something called a Law.

With progress and machines come many laws. Laws are like stories. Most fade and die because they are bad laws, or weak. A few, too few, are good because they keep alive what is true and protect what is right. In some deep place there are those who remember the sacred Earth. They wish to protect what remains.

This is one of these laws—a good one. It declares that no eagle, in the process of building or maintaining a nest, can be "disturbed or agitated in any way that might cause injury, decrease its productivity, interfere with breeding, feeding, or sheltering behavior, or in any way lead to nest abandonment."

In this world this is the law. The penalties for breaking this law are extremely harsh. The marsh must be protected and be restored so that the nest will thrive. The falling water will once again fill and spill over the Cradle of Stone.

So just now a man with a notebook and a hard hat looks up at the eagle, and she looks down upon him. He shakes his head and walks to a place halfway between tree and machine. He draws his hand across his throat. One by one the engines sputter to a stop. And then—silence.

Again there is the slam of doors and the men depart. They will return for the machinery another day.

The boy lifts his hand from the shallow print—so shallow now he has to look hard to see it. But there it is—the stone image of a hand. Before the boy was free to wonder whose hand it was that made the print or why it was here…or...

A soft chattering high in the tree draws his eyes to the mother. First her one eye, then the other, fix upon his. He smiles. It might be she smiles as well. With an eagle, it is hard to tell.

What is important is that her eyes tell him she knows him—his eyes that he knows her, though they have never met. Things happen that way sometimes. And it is good they do.

And so the heart of a new story, born of the old, has been told.

NOTES AND GLOSSARY

Alonqua's tribe is the Lenni Lenape which means "Common" or "Ordinary People." The Lenape, through recorded history, have lived mainly in what is now Eastern Pennsylvania, Delaware, and New Jersey. In the late 1600's, the Lenni Lenape, also known as the Delaware, enjoyed a generally harmonious relationship with the white settlers, largely due to the great respect paid to the Tribe by the founder of the Pennsylvania colony, William Penn. The relationship went sour after Penn's death.

Under the auspices of his sons, the Lenape were forced in 1737 to cede a great tract of land as a result of what is known as the Walking Purchase. The Lenape agreed to give up an amount of land that could be walked in a day and a half. Penn's son hired trained runners who covered nearly seventy miles in that time span. Forced to give up more than five times the amount of land expected, the majority of the Lenape left and headed west. They arrived in North Central Ohio and settled most densely along the northern tributaries of the Muskingum River. Here there was rich land, good hunting, and relative peace for two generations. Many believed that they had returned to their ancient home, and that they had hunted the mastodons here at the time of the glaciers more than 10,000 years ago.

The Lenape lived there until the Revolutionary War, trying to stay neutral, even leaning toward the American side, while most other tribes supported the British. When America emerged victorious, any benefits of Lenape support soon faded in the wake of hordes of settlers seeking cheap land. The rise of the Shawnee chief, Tecumseh, sparked many Delaware to fight for their land, but after his death in 1811, hope was lost and they left the Ohio lands. The tribe first resettled in Indiana, but were soon forced to move on. One branch turned to the north and on into Canada, the other to the southwest, and finally into Oklahoma. These two branches, along with a remnant population in eastern Pennsylvania, comprise the majority of the Lenape living today.

The Lenape Way

That the Tribe called itself the "common people" reveals much about them and what can be referred to as "the Lenape Way." It is also why I have been so deeply drawn to the people and their culture. A Lenape friend of mine once told me the Lenape Way is "the natural path of human beings untainted by any aspects of a dominant culture." Not only do these "common people" not place any human being above or below another, consider what a Lenape chief said to an army officer who had come to a village in order to offer a treaty. When asked by the officer how many lived in the village, the Chief responded by saying he had no way of knowing for certain. It would take too long to count the trees and the animals who were seen as equal members.

My friend went on to say the Lenape Way asks that our inner rhythms join the rhythms of the Earth. He says, "Birds sing, so we learn to sing. Trees are still, so we learn to be still. Storms cleanse the air, we learn to do the same. Deer listen intently, we learn to listen intently. We learn from all that is around us, because all are one."

The Lenape Way, then, is all about connections, the way all parts of creation mesh and resonate with each other. It is also about connecting past, present, and future, and how, at any moment we are, who we were, who we are, and who we will be. It is the Lenape Way that animates and shapes Alonqua's story. And it is the Lenape Way that connects one boy of two hundred years ago to a boy of our time—and to a boy of the Ice Age.

The Lenape Way emphasizes that nothing natural is ordinary, that all of creation is sacred. Given that their "village" includes the trees and animals, Alonqua sees these entities, even "inanimate" objects, as living equals and he addresses them as such.

The Lenape Language

Several years ago when I embarked upon the journey of *The Cradle of Stone*, I attended a Lenape language conference at Swarthmore College. The main thrust of the gathering was to remove the Lenape language from linguists' books, place it into the mouths of tribal people, and bring it to life. The language had become as scattered as the people. The Munsee branch, whose Trail of Tears took them to Canada, the Unami branch who went to Oklahoma, and the Eastern Lenape who more fully assimilated and settled in the ancestral home of Pennsylvania, found that both words and syntax had diverged greatly. The three central issues at the conference focused on unifying the language into one form understood by all tribal members, teaching the language, particularly to the young people, and using the language in everyday living.

The most moving aspect of this conference to me was the prevailing idea that the Lenape language was a direct expression of the soul of the people. And it was clear that without the language, the People could not articulate how they viewed the world, and that the unique perspective that is Lenape was being lost. I learned the language is rich and highly complex, but that at its root is its direct ties with experience which gives the words and syntax a sense of immediacy and vitality. Colors such as red and blue are not nouns or adjectives, but actions that express blueness or redness. Actions themselves are more important than the agents of the actions, as pronouns are embedded within the verb form. An everyday activity, such as "using the bathroom," is expressed refreshingly as "must go hide quickly."

There is also a strong poetic element to many words and phrases. For example, the moon is referred to as *"piskeweni kishux"* which means "sun of the night." *"Weski Kishux,"* the crescent moon, is translated as "moon of a little while ago."

By far the largest category of Lenape words used in this story is animal. This was an easy decision. To compare the sound of these words with their English counterpart leaves one with the impression that the Lenape were so close to these animals that their words for them seem to be a direct extension of the animal, itself. Consider *pamputis* and snapping turtle, *kwenoomuk* and otter, *kwikwinkum* and duck, or *temakwe* and beaver. The Lenape names conjure up visions of the animal, not only in appearance but behavior and even personality. This emphasizes the Lenape view that all of creation lives on one level, and that all is connected through *Kishelamukong*, the Spirit Who Created the Universe in Thought. It is clear that the language and the people are one. *Is* Kishelamukong *a who or a what?*

Lenape Pronunciation

No attempt is made in the glossary to offer pronunciation for the words. There are online Lenape phonic guides for those who need precision. The words sound strange, but the letters correspond generally to the English language. A few general points can be made, however. The letter "i" has a long "e" sound, "u" is "oo," "a" is pronounced "ah", and "e" is long "a." Many Lenape words end in "w," suggesting the "w" sound followed by the briefest "uh" sound. For example, the Lenape word for "star" is *"alonqw.*" For such words ending with "w" I have substituted "ua" or "we." So *"alonqw"* becomes *"alonqua;" "temak*w" becomes *"temakwe."* In the case of the Guardian Spirit, the "w" at the end of *"Mesingw"* is silent, so the true spelling remains in the story. This reflects what is sometimes done with contemporary tribal members to facilitate the flow of the written language.

I have translated most Lenape words simply with their English counterpart. Some words, however, demand more attention. Such words as *"opalanie"* (eagle) and *"sippu"* (river) hold sacred meanings that need to be explored. In addition, I was unable to find Lenape equivalents for some words and names. An example would be *"Sikon Taleka;"* literally it means "singers of spring," but it refers to the spring peeper. I found no Lenape name for this delightful creature, so I put a name together. This is not an attempt to play "fast and loose" with the language, but to find a way to fill in a blank while adhering to the spirit of the language and the people.

To use Lenape words in this story is not an attempt to reanimate the language. The purpose is to raise an awareness of the richness and beauty of the Lenape culture and worldview. It is hoped in turn this will awaken in the reader his or her own need to reconnect with this Earth. We live in a time that pulls us away from a living, breathing relationship with our true home, which even as we deny it through our modern lifestyle, is a deep part of our true selves.

Glossary

Due to the divergence of the people and the language, words used in this glossary may not be universally agreed upon by every speaker of the language.

Animal Names

Chihokepelis: Bluebird
Chulens: Bird
Ghokos: Owl
Kwenoomuk: Otter
Kwuswukis: Killdeer
Names: fish
Pamputis: Snapping Turtle
Pipisilunkon: Bat
Opalanie: Bald Eagle

The Lenape, like many Native American tribes, revere the eagle. Its wings take it higher and its eyes see more than other living creature. Seen as a messenger between earth and heaven, it embodies balance and spirituality. There is no more powerful animal totem, and anyone whose spirit is touched by eagle medicine is called upon to connect human hearts to eternal truth.

Temakwe: Beaver
Xalaputis: Spider

The spider is considered by many Native American tribes to be the storyweaver, a mysterious presence whose web suggests the intricate art of storytelling.

Xanhanni: Frog

The frog might seem weak and vulnerable, but to the Lenape its power equals that of the eagle. It is the bringer and protector of new life. Like the eagle it is a connector of two worlds: water and earth. Its presence is a sign of prevailing hope and renewal.

Xanikwe: Squirrel

Trees and Plants

Apawiak: Cattail (Root eaten raw or cooked)
Ansikeme: Maple Tree

The Lenape people for centuries have gathered the sweet sap from this tree and boiled it down into syrup and sugar. This method is briefly described in Chapter 10.

*Ashikemensh*a: Fern
Otaes: Spring Beauty (wildflower with edible tubers)
Wanikwe: Sassafras tree

It is a traditional belief among the Lenape that tea brewed from the root of this tree is sacred. When the roots are gathered just before the first spring storm there is great power in this drink.

Xaxakwe: Sycamore tree

Natural Objects and Places

Ahsen: Stone
Aptachuteh: Place of the Frozen Heart
Aspitunk Pilsu: High Place of the Pure Heart
Piskweni Kishux: Moon (Sun of the Night)
Sippu: River

To the Lenape, as to other tribes, the river is sacred. Its eternal flowing speaks of timelessness. If one wishes to speak to an ancestor, he or she stands in the river and faces upstream. If one wishes to speak to the future he or she faces downstream to where the water is flowing.

Sukpehelak: Waterfall
Weski Kishux: New Moon (Moon of a Little While Ago)

People

Alonqua: Star (also *Sapelei Opalanie:* Shining Eagle, Alonqua's spirit name)
Mawenteh: Heart Gatherer
Pishkwa: Chief Nighthawk

Temetet: Little Wolf (Teme is the word for wolf)

Deities

Kishelamukong: Creator (Who Has Created the Universe in Thought)

Manito or Gitchi Manito: Great Spirit Which Flows Through all of Creation

Mesingw: Guardian Spirit of the Forest, also known as The Living Solid Face

Common Words and Phrases

Lapich Knewell: I will see you again (There is no direct "goodbye" equivalent in Lenape)

Newichema: Help him

Owapicnoway: I will not see you for a long time.

Nihmat: Brother (*Nihmates:* Brothers)

Wanishi: Thank you

Yukwe: Now

Weli Kishku: Good day, or it is a good day

www.ingramcontent.com/pod-product-compliance
Lightning Source LLC
Chambersburg PA
CBHW030520310726
48979CB00010B/1741/J

* 9 7 8 0 9 9 9 4 6 2 3 0 0 *